A PICTURE OF HAPPINESS

Araminta Shaw was a country girl. Steven Lewis was a town boy. They met at the auction of Araminta's grandfather's home, Thornclough Manor. Steven was hoping to buy the house for a pop star, and Araminta was searching for a valuable family portrait belonging to her mother. The last thing Araminta expected to find was love. But could a relationship between two people from very different backgrounds ever work?

Books by Louise Armstrong
in the Linford Romance Library:

HOLD ON TO PARADISE
JAPANESE MAGIC

LOUISE ARMSTRONG

A PICTURE OF HAPPINESS

Complete and Unabridged

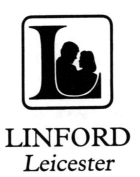

LINFORD
Leicester

First published in Great Britain
under the name of 'Louise Strong'

First Linford Edition
published 2001

Copyright © 1999 by Louise Strong

British Library CIP Data

Armstrong, Louise
A picture of happiness.—Large print ed.—
Linford romance library
1. Love stories
2. Large type books
I. Title
823.9′14 [F]

ISBN 0–7089–4565–1

Published by
F. A. Thorpe (Publishing)
Anstey, Leicestershire

Set by Words & Graphics Ltd.
Anstey, Leicestershire
Printed and bound in Great Britain by
T. J. International Ltd., Padstow, Cornwall

This book is printed on acid-free paper

1

It was the most perfect spring day imaginable. An enormous blue sky hung over the bulk of Pendle Hill, with only a few clouds floating against the blue. Fresh green buds sprouted in all the hedgerows, and birds flitted through the greenery.

Yet Araminta Shaw was as miserable as she had ever been in her life.

'I must be crazy,' she muttered under her breath.

She pushed up the sleeves of her green waxed jacket, the way she always did when she was nervous, but she kept walking up the sweep of gravel drive that led to Thornclough Manor. Despite the sunshine, the air was Lancashire-cold. She half-wished she had put on a scarf, if not for the cold, at least to stop her curls blowing irritatingly into her face.

In her twenties now, she took for granted her slim figure and creamy skin. If she looked in a mirror it was only to frown briefly at her freckles before cleaning her teeth.

It never occurred to her to admire her high cheekbones and tip-tilted chin. She had been too thoroughly teased as a younger girl about her freckles to ever see herself as pretty, and she was unaware how lovely people thought her. She rarely gave her appearance a second thought.

Today, as she walked along the drive, she was absorbed in thoughts about the house that was coming into view. It was a Georgian delight. Built from local stone, with an enchanting pillared porch and perfectly proportioned windows, the house looked as if it was just waiting for a camera crew to turn up and film a Jane Austen novel around its timeless beauty.

Only the production team would have a lot of work to do before they could make people believe the house was lived in. A closer inspection showed that dandelions were blooming in the gravel drive. The paint on the beautiful windows had peeled down to the bare wood and slipped tiles in the roof above had led to wet patches in the walls below. The house bore all the signs of long neglect.

There was quite a scattering of cars parked on the gravel in front of the house — a dark green Range Rover that looked new, two estates, an ancient, red open-backed wagon, a couple of mid-range models and a battered Mini. The various car owners were standing around the house. Most of them were looking at it with identical expressions of denigration.

A woman in a sheepskin jacket prodded one of the window frames with a screwdriver. What she found there made her screw up her vivid lip-sticked mouth and shake her head in disgust. As Araminta slowed to a hesitant stop on the gravel, wondering whether she should just turn tail and run home, the woman in the sheepskin jacket shouted over to a tall man in a tweed jacket.

'You'll never sell this pile! I'm not even going to make you an offer,' she called out.

The man in the tweed jacket shrugged his shoulders. He was setting up a folding table in front of the entrance and setting out his papers. Araminta realised that he must be the auctioneer.

'I have to go through the motions,' he pointed out. 'The land is immensely valuable, and if nothing else, there's some good scrap to be had out of the house.'

Scrap! Araminta swallowed hard. This was worse than she had imagined! She had never even been inside the building, but a pain knifed through her heart as she imagined a wrecker's ball smashing the house into nothing. If only she'd been able to raise the money!

She'd tried hard enough. How many

practical, level-headed, profit-minded, sharp-eyed mortgage advisors and loan officers had heard her stumbling request and shaken their heads over her meagre account books? Enough to give her nightmares.

No-one was prepared to lend money to a self-employed, stained-glass artist who made well under the minimum wage. Araminta could hardly blame them, because even as she'd asked for a loan, she'd known that she'd have trouble paying it back. Yet she'd felt impelled to try, just as she felt impelled to be here today.

Only now she wished she hadn't come because she was going to see Thornclough Manor sold for scrap! Her gaze turned to a burly man in a filthy duffel coat who was leaning on the red wagon and smoking a hand-rolled cigarette. Clearly visible under the grime that coated the wagon's doors were the words: T. Nutter & Sons. Reclaimed stone and timber.

'It's a shame when these old places

are let go,' a man said who looked like a farmer.

Araminta noticed that people were drifting up, naturally grouping themselves around the man in the tweed jacket. It was nearly time for the auction to begin.

'What's the story on this one?' someone asked.

'Usual thing,' the woman in the sheepskin jacket said. 'The owner got too frail to keep it up, and then the stubborn old codger was in a nursing home for twenty years before he finally died. But he wouldn't let the place go, wouldn't admit that he'd never be well enough to return to it. Didn't want strangers in it, and so it just began to fall apart.'

'Old fool,' one of the listeners said unsympathetically, but even as Araminta winced to hear her grandfather described so, a deep, smoky voice came from behind her.

'He was a generous old fool at any rate. Did you know that he owned most of the village? And when he died he left all the property to whoever was renting it at the time?'

'No!' several of the people exclaimed.

They were now grouped loosely on the gravel waiting for the auction to begin. The woman in the sheepskin coat spoke for them all.

'Better than winning the lottery! Thornclough is one of the prettiest villages in Lancashire, and the houses must be worth thousands. Lucky, lucky people!'

As the topic of conversation changed from the eccentricities of her grandfather to the luck of the people who had benefited from his will, Araminta stole a look at the man who had changed the subject. He was breathtaking enough to distract her from her problems.

He was tall, muscled, dark blond. He was bantering with the sheepskin-jacketed woman now, showing very white teeth and a persuasive smile. Araminta heard the woman call him Steven, so she guessed they must sometimes meet at house auctions, and from their conversation it was obvious that he was in the business. There was an attraction about him that made her keep eavesdropping, and watching.

Thick black lashes bristled around grey eyes that seemed to brim over with light and laughter. A neat, orderly air about his well-cut suit and highly-polished shoes, together with an indefinable aura of capability and command, made Araminta think that he might have been in the army at some time. His dark blond hair was well cut, and the suit he wore was so easily in the height of fashion. His accent wasn't local, and Araminta moved closer, wondering where he was from.

Just as the man in the tweed jacket banged his gavel and announced the beginning of the auction, Steven turned his head and noticed Araminta. He gave her a long, hard look. It had so much appreciation in it that she felt hot blood sting her cheeks, and she had to turn away from him. Yet she knew he was still looking at her. She was strangely aware of him.

Over the sounds of general movement, as people jostled for the best place around the auctioneer, Araminta heard his feet crunching over the gravel towards her. It was an effort to look up and meet his clear-eyed gaze. It was unnerving to see the admiration in his expression.

'Hello,' he said, smiling and holding out his hand to her. 'I haven't met you at an auction before, but if you're in the business, we're bound to meet again. I'm Steven Lewis.'

Araminta took his hand. His skin felt warm and his grip was strong and friendly. She heard herself stammering stupidly with nerves.

'A-Araminta Shaw. I'm not in the business at all.'

Her knees felt shaky and her heartbeat was erratic. She wished she could think of something sophisticated to say, but this smiling, handsome man unnerved her dreadfully. She wasn't used to taking to attractive men.

She dropped his hand, half expecting him to turn his attention away from her to the auction. But he ignored the auctioneer's chanting description of the property for sale and stood next to Araminta and smiled down at her gently.

'You're just taking an interest?'

'Yes. No. That is, I live in the village,' Araminta managed to say, amazed at the effect this stranger was having on her.

2

The auctioneer's chant rose to a frenzy as he begged for opening bids. It was Araminta who broke the eye contact with the stranger. Her attention slid away and fixed itself upon the sale. The woman in the sheepskin jacket made the opening bid. Her offer was topped by a man who looked like a farmer, and then, to Araminta's horror, that offer was topped by the stone merchant.

Araminta was clenching her hands so tightly that, later in the day when she took her evening bath, she found crescent-shaped nail marks in the palms of her hands, but for now she was completely unaware of the pain. Her whole being was following the progress of the sale as the woman in the sheepskin jacket made another bid.

The auctioneer tried to whip up some enthusiasm in the crowd, but most of them soon dropped out, shaking their heads regretfully. Araminta knew some of the locals. They had come along, just in case the manor went for such a low price that they could afford to buy it for the land alone, but the woman in the sheepskin jacket took the bidding over what the local farmers were willing to pay, and one by one they stopped bidding. Soon, despite the auctioneer's best efforts, so did the woman in the sheepskin jacket.

'That's my limit for the dump,' she called cheerfully.

The auctioneer, who obviously knew her well, leaned over to her and replied, 'You don't know a bargain when you see one!' before turning to the stone merchant. 'Looks like your lucky day, Mr Nutter,' he observed informally. 'Going once,' he chanted, 'going twice . . .'

Araminta shuddered all over. Thornclough Manor was to be destroyed, and with it, her precious heirloom — the only personal possession her mother had been left with after the split with her family. Araminta's parents had told her the old story without bitterness. They were sad about the rift, but cared nothing for wealth. Even when Araminta's father died, she and her mother had still had each other.

It was only when she had realised that her illness was terminal that Araminta's mother had thought of her heirloom with sudden urgency.

'It's the only valuable thing I can leave you, darling,' she had said. 'I'm so sorry now that I put off reclaiming it, but I thought there would be plenty of time.'

The thin hands had plucked restlessly at the bed cover.

'I was wrong. I should have taken better care of you.'

The worried frown between her mother's brows hurt Araminta. She put her arms around the thin figure.

'You've taken perfect care of me,' she assured her mother. 'And all without help from your family. Even after

Daddy died, we managed. You made a home for both of us. You got me through art college. Don't worry about it now.'

'But I want you to have it,' her mother insisted. 'I want to be sure that you'll be all right when I'm gone. It's not just that I want you to own the painting, beautiful as it is, but it worries me that you've no resources. Find Camille's letter. Get the painting back, Araminta. Promise me. You've nothing put by for a rainy day, and I won't be here to look after you. I can't bear to think of you needing money and having no way to raise it.'

Araminta had looked out the letter from Camille Barton, an artist who was now so famous that even a letter written by her was probably valuable because of the signature, and read the contents out loud to her mother.

I'm afraid I didn't get very far with your father at all, darling. He blames me because I introduced you to your husband, which, whatever your father

14

may say, I will never regret, because there never was a happier couple than you and Alex.

Of course, darling Alex is the typical poor artist and will never make a dime in his life, but all the money in the world wouldn't have made up for you marrying the farmer your father had lined up for you. Anyway, I didn't manage to persuade him to even let me into the house, let alone reclaim my portrait of you, and I'm off to Africa now on an extended painting trip so you will have to think up some other way of getting our picture back.

And it is yours. I did it for you, as a gift. Don't let anyone talk you out of your ownership. The way prices are for my work at present you would be able to retire on the proceeds of that painting, which gives me great satisfaction as you and darling Alex will never let me help you.

But anyway, darling, the picture is yours and I want you to have it. There must be some way to reclaim it. All the *best to you and baby Araminta. See you when I get back from Africa.*

'Poor Camille,' her mother whispered. 'All that talent. All that beauty.'

Araminta had often heard the story from her mother and she smiled as she tenderly folded the precious letter yet again.

'Put it away safely, darling,' her mother said. 'You'll need it as proof of ownership.'

And she had made Araminta promise to retrieve the painting from her grandfather's home in Lancashire, which was why Araminta had settled in the village of Thornclough.

★ ★ ★

She still missed her mother, but her life as a stained-glass artist was deeply satisfying. Commissions were beginning to trickle in, and she did a surprisingly brisk trade when she opened her little workshop to the public on Sundays.

People liked the delicate artistry of

her vases, lamps and screens. Knowing only too well that not everyone could afford large pieces, she also made sun-catchers and glass mobiles to bring light and movement to people's windows. Such customers frequently returned, remarking that her work had given them so much pleasure they had saved up for a larger piece, or even decided to install a whole window.

She was now beginning to feel secure in her ability to make a living the way she wanted to. The rent on her cottage and stone barn workshop was paid. She lived frugally, but comfortably, and there was even a tiny nest egg beginning to mount up in the bank. What she hadn't been able to achieve was anything like the sum needed to buy Thornclough Manor, and now it was being sold to . . .

Steven Lewis stirred beside her and raised a hand.

'I'll raise that bid,' he called.

The stone merchant looked furious.

'I hope you've got a realistic idea of

demolition costs,' he said nastily, raising the bid again. 'I'll hardly raise a profit myself at this price, and I've got all my own equipment.'

Araminta's heart beat faster as Steven raised the bid once more before looking at Mr Nutter.

'Thanks for your advice,' he drawled lazily. 'But my client doesn't want the house demolished. And he won't care what he spends on it.'

Araminta's heart gave a great leap. Not demolished. Her eyes flew to Steven's face. He was calmly eyeing the stone merchant, who was staring back through narrowed eyes, clearly wondering if Steven was bluffing.

'You're trying to pull my leg, trick me into dropping out,' Mr Nutter snarled. 'Who'd spend money on this place?'

'Fred Sparkle,' Steven replied calmly.

A ripple of interest ran through the crowd. There was something about Steven's very presence that made them inclined to believe him, but as well as that, the hottest story in the Press right now was the young pop star's public admittance of his troubles with alcohol and his intention to step out of the public eye.

Araminta had read an interview with Fred Sparkle in a recent Sunday newspaper. He had declared that he wanted to find a quiet place in the country where he could recover and concentrate on his song writing. She had just never expected that quiet place to be Thornclough Manor.

Steven's bombshell settled the matter. The auction was over. Mr Nutter tossed aside his home-made cigarette, stamped over to his red wagon, and disappeared in a noxious cloud of diesel fumes. The other disappointed buyers drifted towards their cars, pausing only briefly to discuss the amazing turn of events.

Araminta stood digging her feet into the gravel, wondering what on earth she should do next.

3

Araminta heard Steven Lewis say to the auctioneer, 'I always bring a flask to these things. Will you have a coffee with me while we sign the papers?'

The auctioneer smiled gratefully.

'I'm freezing,' he admitted. 'I'd love a hot drink.'

As the last car doors slammed and the last engine droned down the drive, Araminta was the only person left standing around. She had just decided that she had better leave, too, when Steven strode over and stood smiling down at her. The warmth in his vivid grey eyes made her nervous.

'Will you have coffee with us?' he invited softly.

Araminta's eyelashes fluttered down over her eyes in a reflex defence against his maleness, but she managed to say calmly, 'Thank you. I'd love one.'

She moved over to stand next to the tweed-clad auctioneer, almost as if he would protect her, from what she didn't know. Steven went over to the green Range Rover and opened the boot. He returned bearing a large Thermos flask. Steven drank from the cap of his flask and gave Araminta and the auctioneer a smart picnic cup each. The coffee tasted hot, strong, fragrant.

As the two men dealt with the paperwork, Araminta stood holding her drink, feeling awkward. She knew she should seize this golden opportunity to talk with the new owner of Thornclough Manor, or rather his agent, but she was also fighting a strong urge to run away. The impulse to flee grew stronger as the auctioneer packed away his papers and folding table and drove away.

The cup was shaking in her hand as Steven moved towards her.

'Are you interested in old houses?'

Araminta heard herself replying calmly, 'Yes, but this one in particular.

21

You see, Mr Shaw was my grandfather.'

Steven's well-shaped brows lifted over his expressive eyes.

'Grandfather! Then why . . . ?'

He choked off the question that had sprung to his lips.

'I'm sorry. It's no business of mine.'

'It is in a way. You see — ' Araminta broke off. 'I'm afraid it's a long story. I do want to talk to you about it, and ask you something, but do you have time?'

Steven looked at his watch, but absently, as if it was an automatic gesture, then he looked back at her with a smile in his eyes.

'Actually, I was going to take a quick look at the old place. Will you come with me? I need to size it up. I haven't yet decided which architect to engage.'

'Wouldn't Fred Sparkle decide that?' Araminta asked.

Steven inserted a huge, iron key into the stubborn old lock and then exerted all his strength to push open the door.

'He's leaving all that to me. I know what he wants, and I'll do my best to have it ready for him when he comes out of the clinic he is in at present.'

The door opened with a bang and a gust of old plaster and stale air.

'Pooh!' Araminta said, wrinkling her nose. 'Age and neglect.'

'Damp,' Steven said, more technically. 'Only to be expected after being empty for so long.'

And then he turned to Araminta with open curiosity in his grey eyes.

'Have you never been here before?'

'Never. Grandfather quarrelled with my mother,' Araminta explained as she crossed the threshold and followed Steven into the house.

What had once been charmingly-striped Regency wallpaper hung in strips from every wall that she could see, and dust-laden cobwebs drifted from every corner, picture rail and the curving wooden staircase. Yet, despite the neglect, Araminta thought that the house felt warm and inviting, as if it was welcoming them inside, eager for company after so long.

Araminta closed her eyes for a moment and savoured the reality of being inside Thornclough Manor. Then she remembered her companion and hastened to continue her family history.

'Grandfather objected to the poor artist whom my mother wanted to marry. I'm afraid he was very old-fashioned, and so angry when she defied him that he never forgave her. He tore up her letters, refused to see her. I remember when I was very young, when we first heard that Grandfather was ill and in a nursing home, my mother took me to see him.'

'Go on,' Steven prompted.

He had whipped out a shorthand notebook and was scribbling notes, presumably about the house, but Araminta saw that he was listening to her at the same time.

'Grandfather threw us out,' she continued. 'Mother spoke with the matron every year, but the old man never weakened, never sent for her. The terrible irony is that she died before him, but he never even sent word even then.'

Steven looked up sharply.

'Your mother died?'

Araminta nodded, feeling the gnawing hurt that always came with the thought.

'I'm sorry.'

The very simplicity of his words soothed her.

'Thank you. I miss her.'

'And you never met your grandfather?'

She shook her head.

'I'm sorry about that, too. Families should stick together. I've finished in here. Do you mind if we keep moving?'

Araminta followed Steven into a very neglected dining-room. Despite the rot and dirt, the same air of warmth and welcome was palpable. Its lovely proportions made her fingers itch to pick up a broom and sweep away all the debris. When Araminta didn't continue her story, Steven prompted her gently.

'Your father? The poor artist?'

Araminta watched him for a minute. He seemed to be listing the furniture in his notebook. Even under the layers of dust that coated the wood, Araminta could see water damage, but like the room, there was an intrinsic quality to the furniture that made her yearn to restore it, although it would be a big job.

The fabric of the backs and seats of the dining chairs were so rotten that one panel disintegrated in a puff of dust as Steven touched it with one exploratory finger.

'I'm not dressed for this,' he grimaced, brushing dust off his immaculate suit. 'I'll bring jeans next time. Anyway, what happened to your father, Araminta?'

'My father died long ago,' she said, moving over to one of the long windows that were set along the length of the room.

Each window framed the most delightful view. Araminta realised that the house had been positioned so that it looked over the roofs of the village and across to the great moorland bulk of Pendle Hill. She pushed a dusty curtain to one side and craned her head, wondering if she could pick out the roof of her workshop. Rotten curtain fabric ripped under her fingers. She jumped back hastily.

'Sorry about that.'

Steven paused in his scribbling and gave her a smile that set her heart thudding again.

'Don't worry. There's no chance of preserving any of the original curtains or carpets. You can't do any more damage than time has already done.'

He turned back to his listing. There was an underlying warmth and sympathy in his voice that stripped his next remark of any mockery it might have held.

'So you're an orphan now. Are you poor as well?'

Araminta laughed.

'As poor as my father! I'm an artist, too. I've got enough, but nothing valuable, except for . . . '

She paused. How to explain? Araminta felt hot blood sting her cheeks as she met Steven's cool but interested gaze. She realised that he might think her a vulture, swooping in after her grandfather's death, picking over the remains.

She suddenly wished that she'd never come into the house with him. More! She wished that she'd never promised her mother that she would retrieve the heirloom, or move to Thornclough, or having begun the long chain of events that had directly led to her standing in a freezing cold, derelict, Regency dining-room opposite a strange man with a calm look of enquiry in his eyes.

As the silence lengthened, and their eyes held, Araminta noticed that there was a line of black around the grey irises of Steven's eyes. The artist in her admired the contrast of the dark line against the clear whites. She was so lost in the abstract beauty of his eyes that a shock went through her when the pupils narrowed slightly and he spoke.

'Is this where the story begins? Your grandfather left the bulk of his estate to the nursing home, didn't he? Are you going to contest the will?'

Araminta laughed a little. He'd made it easy for her.

'Certainly not! The matron there looked after him for twenty years. She deserves every penny. No, there's only one thing that I want, one thing that I'm entitled to, and nobody knows where that is. In fact, Grandfather may even have destroyed it.'

'Destroyed?'

Steven's dark brows lifted as he ushered Araminta before him through the double doors that connected the dining-room to a long, light drawing-room. Araminta exclaimed aloud over the beauty of the moulded ceiling and the wood panelling that graced the walls. But as with the rest of the house, dirt and decay blotted out the perfection of the room. A flash of movement in the far corner drew Araminta's eye to a broken glass pane in the top of one of the tall windows.

'Swallows,' she gasped. 'They've come inside to nest under the panelling.'

Steven moved past her to look up at the cup-shaped nest that was attached to the top of a beautifully-carved panel then down to the mess that the birds had made on the floor under it.

'Swallows, and what I shall politely refer to as swallow debris,' he said, shaking his head. 'From the size of this pile of, er, swallow debris, they must have been coming here for years.'

He made a note on his pad.

'Perhaps we could fit them a nesting box just outside the window.'

Araminta liked his thought for the birds. It gave her the courage to answer him freely when he prompted her once more.

'You were telling me about this mysterious family possession. What is it exactly?'

'A painting, by Camille Barton.'

He spun on his heel and his grey eyes met her brown ones with stunning impact.

'Camille Barton? **The** Camille Barton? Why, one of her pictures was auctioned for a fortune last month. Didn't you hear about it?'

Araminta pushed back her curls.

'Of course I did. She was a friend of my mother's, so I always take an interest in her.'

Steven put his notebook in his jacket pocket.

'A genuine Camille Barton would be worth more than the manor, several times more. Are you trying to tell me that there's one of her paintings somewhere in this house, and it's yours?'

'I suppose I am,' Araminta said, feeling guilty for some reason. 'You see, Camille was staying with mother, and it was Camille who introduced my mother to my father. Camille was so pleased when the pair of them fell in love that she did a picture as an

31

engagement present.'

'If the painting was hers, why didn't your mother take it with her?' Steven asked.

'She couldn't,' Araminta explained. 'Grandfather was so furious that she did the classic escape in the middle of the night. She only took what she could carry, and she never came back.'

Steven was frowning.

'This is a strange story. I see your interest now. You want access to the house to retrieve your property.'

He frowned again, working out the implications.

'You'll have to forgive me for this question, Araminta, but my client will want to know, and possibly take legal advice on the matter. Do you have proof of ownership?'

'Oh, yes, several times over. There are documents written by Camille, in fact she mentioned it again in her will, and my mother left it to me in her will. The picture has never been exhibited, of course, or even photographed, but its history, and ownership, is well documented. Every time there's been a major exhibition of Camille's work, an official approach has been made to Grandfather, but he always refused to hand the picture over. Short of taking legal action, or forcing her way into the manor, which mother would never do, there was no way of making him give us the picture.'

Steven was smiling now, his grey eyes light and deliciously friendly.

'It sounds as if you'll have no problem there. You must understand that I'll have to consult Fred Sparkle, or more probably his lawyers, before I can give you access to the house, but I'll see what I can do.'

'Thank you,' Araminta said gratefully.

She realised that she hadn't even had to ask Steven for the favour. He had divined her need and offered to help her. She couldn't help wondering about him as she followed his broad back into the most beautiful, but also the saddest, room she had ever seen in her life.

'The books!' she cried in dismay. 'All the books are ruined.'

Steven nodded in agreement.

'I'll get an expert up just in case there's anything to be salvaged,' he said sadly, 'but I'm very much afraid you are right. This library is past restoration.'

A great patch of plaster had come away from the ceiling in the centre of the room, bringing away with it the massive central chandelier. The rows of library shelves were so coated with debris that the books that lined them were visible only as plaster-coated bumps.

Araminta looked around her sadly. The smell of damp was much stronger in this room, and ominous wet streaks rippled over the ceiling and down the walls. Yet, like the rest of the house, underneath the dirt and decay, a beautiful personality called out to her, and she longed to make it better. Then her professional attention was caught by the most striking feature of the library.

'Look at that glass panel,' she breathed.

Plastered into the wall above the fireplace, taking up the whole wall of the chimney breast, was a huge, dirty and broken slab of stained and leaded glass. It was a fabulously old-fashioned map of the world. It had mountains and rivers and smoking volcanoes. The oceans were decorated with billowing waves and sailing ships mixed with sporting dolphins and spouting whales. The four winds blew from each corner and a fat, jolly sun smiled down over his empire.

Araminta went to it and stood on tiptoes to run loving fingertips over the bottom part of the leaded panel.

'It's the most unusual glass. I wonder if it was a Tiffany design.'

'What? That old thing?' Steven said. 'It's just a bit of dark, old glass and very broken. I think it looks strange up there over the fire. Pointless.'

Araminta turned to him with her eyes glowing.

'There would have been a light inside it. Can't you imagine it lit up from behind, all the colours glowing like jewels?'

'Not really,' Steven admitted. 'It's terribly broken, so I don't suppose we ever will see it like that. Fred will want to scrap it. He has very definite ideas about style.'

'No! He mustn't scrap it. It can be restored.'

Steven was shaking his head, a little regretfully.

'I can see it means a lot to you, but even if the architect could work stained-glass into Fred's design scheme, I'd have to warn him that the panel would need hundreds of hours of skilled, and that means expensive, labour.'

'I'll do it,' Araminta rushed in impulsively. 'I'm a stained-glass artist. I'll do it for nothing.'

Steven regarded her with a puzzled expression.

'Why? Why should you do that?'

It was difficult to express her feelings of wanting to love and care for this house, feelings that had crystallised into a rush of determination when she saw the neglected panel. It was out of her power to restore the house, but glass was her business, and she ached to bring out the beauty and potential that she just knew lay inside the neglect. But her feelings ran too deep to be expressed easily.

'Oh, I'd do it by way of a thank you for letting me hunt for my picture,' she insisted. 'Even if Mr Sparkle doesn't want to keep the panel in the house, he'll be able to sell it to someone who does.'

Steven picked up a glass jewel from the fallen chandelier and rubbed it clean absently.

'Ah, yes, your picture. Where did your grandfather have the painting hung? We should get it away from this damp atmosphere as soon as possible.'

Araminta shook her head.

'He didn't have it on show. No-one

has seen the picture for years, and he wouldn't even admit to still having it in the house. That's why I think he may have destroyed it.'

Steven regarded her gravely.

'Why? Why would he destroy such a valuable painting?'

'Back then, Camille's paintings weren't considered valuable. The critics were only just beginning to appreciate her style by the time she died. Grandfather wouldn't have considered the worth of the painting, only the subject matter.'

His grey eyes bored into hers.

'Which was?'

She swallowed and looked away.

'My mother. It was a beautiful portrait of my mother as a young girl, alight with happiness, radiant with her first love. There's a chance that my grandfather destroyed the painting because he couldn't bear to look at it. Quite a few of mother's friends have looked in all the obvious places, but there's never been any sign of it.'

38

Steven looked down at the crystal he'd been polishing and popped it on to a nearby table.

'Ugh. I'm filthy, and all this has taken longer than I expected. I must leave now, Araminta, but I promise that I won't forget you. In fact I'm captivated, by you and your story.'

His eyes met hers briefly.

'I'll make all the arrangements,' he began.

Araminta felt the impact of his personality like a blow as he rushed on, arranging her life for her. Once again she decided that he must have been in the army. She could just see him bossing a regiment around as he summed up crisply!

'Lawyers, documentation, I'll clear access with Fred. I can't see him objecting, in fact it might interest him — the hunt for the missing painting.'

He smiled down at Araminta and she tried to conquer the queer, breathless feeling that he gave her.

'I'll need to comb every inch of the

house, because there's a chance, just a chance that my grandfather hid it away somewhere.'

Steven was still smiling down at her.

'It's Wednesday today,' he said with crisp efficiency. 'I'm afraid that it will take time to sort out the paperwork, so I can't promise that I'll have it all done by Saturday night, but how about I take you for dinner to report on progress?'

4

Araminta felt even more as if she were having dinner with an army major on Saturday evening. Steven had swept her off to one of the best restaurants in Lancashire. She had named it at random when he asked her where she wanted to go, never having been there, but now she luxuriated in the atmosphere. A poor artist didn't often get to eat in such a place.

As the waiter ushered them to a table, all starched linen and polished silver, Araminta admired the pink water lily lampshades that cast a subdued and flattering glow on the faces of all the diners. She thought the decor was just right.

A few minutes later she discovered that the restaurant people might know their stuff, but they charged for it, too. She raised a horrified face from the menu and stared at Steven apologetically.

'I'm sorry. I'd heard the food here was incredible, but I had no idea that it was so expensive.'

One corner of Steven's mouth lifted in an amused smile, but the grey eyes were steady and kind as he replied, 'Don't give it a thought, Araminta. Call this part of the decadent business world and stop figuring out how many tins of baked beans you could buy. You do eat baked beans, don't you?'

'All the time,' she admitted.

The grey eyes flashed.

'You certainly look well enough on it, and you look especially well tonight. Green suits you.'

'Thank you,' she said.

Steven was looking at her with such warm admiration that she felt flustered, and bent over the menu.

'What are you going to have to eat?' she asked hastily.

Steven swung back in his seat.

'Soup and lobster,' he said with

gusto. 'Lobster dripping with butter and cream and cholesterol, and I don't care a bit. I'm going to enjoy every bite. What are you going to have? Don't you dare order an omelette or anything cheap or anything healthy. We're here to enjoy ourselves tonight.'

Are we, Araminta thought. She felt unsure, off balance. Was this a date or a business meeting? She felt that it was important that she try to keep things on a business footing, yet Steven's enjoyment of the evening was infectious. She cleared her throat.

'I'll have queen scallops and Gruyère cheese,' she decided, 'with a basket of mixed breads.'

'And for your main course?

'That will be my main course.'

Steven's mouth quirked downwards.

'Don't tell me you're dieting.'

Araminta laughed.

'No diet!' she declared. 'I'm saving my all for the sticky toffee pudding. I never have room for three courses.'

To her relief, Steven didn't press her

to eat more than she wanted.

'I'll order a green salad with my soup,' he said. 'You can nibble a leaf or two to be companionable while I eat it. That way no-one will notice that I'm eating twice as much as you are.'

'That's a fair division of the food. You're twice the size that I am,' Araminta pointed out laughing.

Steven gave her a mocking, provocative glance. She looked down quickly. What if he thinks I'm flirting with him? She felt the blush of confusion heating her cheeks once more. Her feelings were so overpowering, so new and so different, that she hardly knew how to deal with them. So she quickly changed the subject.

'I don't usually drink much,' she said, not quite looking at him, 'because of my budget, of course, but it means I'm not used to it. How about you?'

'Well, I do like an occasional drink,' he replied. 'But not when I'm driving. Suppose I order us a glass of wine to go with the meal and sparkling water for the rest?'

He was easy to be with, Araminta reflected. If only she didn't feel so foolishly unnerved by him, this would easily be the nicest date she'd been on in a long time — if it was a date. She still wasn't sure.

'Do you have far to drive tonight?' she asked. 'You must think me very rude, but when we met, we talked so much about my portrait that I don't know anything about you except your name. Where do you live?'

She kept her eyes averted, but the sound of his smoky voice was enough to send shivers down her spine as he answered.

'I live in Manchester, but I have no intention of driving back there tonight.'

A chill ran through Araminta and her head jerked up in alarm. She met lazily amused eyes that seemed to know what she was thinking.

'I've booked a room at the village pub, the Golden Lion,' he continued easily. 'I need to spend time at the manor tomorrow.'

A tight band of nerves seemed to ease around Araminta's chest. She could feel her heart beating so quickly that it was affecting her breathing. It was a relief when the first course arrived and they had plates and drinks to deal with and the food to comment on. It broke up the tension. Why does he do this to me, she wondered. It's not as if he's my first date or anything like that. I do have some experience.

She lived a quiet life at the moment, but that was through choice, while she established her business. Her parents' home had always been full of people, and she had dated a lot, in a friendly way, from quite an early age. Then, at art school, she had fallen in love with a much older man, a painter, and despite her mother's disapproval, Araminta had continued to see him for six months, before she realised he was not right for her. But being with him had given her confidence with the opposite sex.

All that confidence seemed to have deserted her tonight, however, and she felt like a teenager again because of the way Steven was affecting her. Araminta strove to overcome her queer feelings of breathlessness and make conversation.

'Have you ever been in the army?' she asked.

Steven regarded her with an appreciative smile.

'That's very perceptive of you. In fact, I haven't, but both my parents were, so I grew up in a military environment.'

'Both of them? That must have caused some complications.'

'It was difficult sometimes. Still, the army is becoming more modern in its outlook, and they do try to take family matters into consideration when they allocate postings. It was surprising how often my parents managed to be together.'

He forked up a big bite of lobster.

'This is excellent. How is yours?'

'Gorgeous!' Araminta declared, through

a mouthful of rich cheese. 'But what happened to you if they couldn't stay together?'

'I stayed with my mother when I was younger, then later I went to boarding school.'

Araminta thought of her own noisy, chaotic, but totally loving parents. She couldn't imagine being parted from them when she was young.

'How was boarding school?' she asked cautiously.

Steven laughed.

'I loved it! Oh, I know it's fashionable at the moment to claim that school was the ruin of you, but mine was terrific, and I was very happy there.'

'I suppose you were used to an institutional life,' Araminta said thoughtfully. 'It wouldn't have been such a big change.'

'And I was consulted about it,' Steven said, pushing away his empty plate. 'Gosh that was good. Once we'd agreed that school was a good idea, my parents took me around several, and I chose the best one.'

'Did you move around a lot?'

'All the time. Hong Kong, Germany, Belize, basically a new place every two years.

Araminta regarded him with awe.

'Think of the packing! It took us three weeks to get ready for a holiday, and when Mother died, emptying the house was a nightmare.'

Steven touched her hand in a brief gesture of sympathy.

'Packing is very different when it is part of your lifestyle,' he assured her. 'Remember, we had a turn-out every two years. You soon get used to travelling light.'

'I don't think I could,' Araminta remarked, thinking of her bulging cupboards at home. 'I could never part with all my treasures.'

Steven smiled at the hovering waiter.

'Sticky toffee pudding for the lady and the strawberry pie is mine, thank you. And could you bring us coffee?'

Then he turned to Araminta.

'Then don't marry an army guy,' he warned her. 'I must admit that I've kept the habit of travelling light, but now my parents have retired, they are turning into pack rats! They've started these huge collections of stamps, coins and antiques. It's amazing how much is crammed into their little bungalow now.'

Araminta stirred her cappuccino.

'Where do they live?'

'Argentina. They like the climate, and an army pension goes a lot further out there.'

'We're both quite alone,' Araminta said.

The words were out before she knew that she was going to say them aloud. It seemed such an intimate comment to make that the blush that seemed to be her constant companion when Steven was around stung her cheeks once more. She had to bend her head over her coffee for a few seconds before she dared look up.

Steven was regarding her with his

most devastating smile, and even as she registered how attractive she found him, he distracted her by leaning forward across the table and changing the subject.

'Here's what I have decided we should do tomorrow.'

5

Despite the steadily-falling rain and the mist-soaked damp that crept in through the open windows of Thornclough Manor, the library seemed full of light and fresh air. Once again, Araminta was convinced that the house was glad to see them, that it was happy to have people moving around it again.

The clang of church bells in the distance broke her train of thought. She put down the broom she had been using and tied the neck of yet another plastic bin sack. She had been filling them with debris all morning.

'Eleven o'clock,' she said, hitting her hands together to knock off the worst of the dust. 'Time for a break.'

'You don't have to do this,' Steven said, switching off the electronic device he was using to measure all the dimensions of the house. 'The builders will clear up when they start the renovation.'

He seemed bigger than ever as he brushed past Araminta to fetch his flask. The faded jeans and red-check shirt he was wearing suited him. Having only seen him in smart and very formal suits, Araminta was surprised just how at home he looked in his casual clothes, and how handsome.

'I know I don't have to clean up,' she said, 'but it helps me to keep things tidy as I search. If I leave a mess, I'll get confused and end up looking in the same place twice. It's better this way.'

They took their coffee over by one of the open windows. Steven motioned Araminta into the window-seat and pulled over a chair for himself.

'A tidy-minded artist,' he said. 'That's unusual.'

'I got teased at art college,' Araminta admitted, 'because I was the only student there with a personal organiser.'

Steven smiled at her, and she was aware of his interest once more. She took a sip of the fragrant black coffee. The damp air by the window was very fresh after the dust of the library, and she felt alive and happy. The church bells gave a few last peals to hurry latecomers.

'I don't know much about you,' Steven said, softly, musingly. 'Do you usually go to church, Araminta?'

'Sometimes,' she answered, 'when I'm not having the day organised around me, that is.'

And then she was suddenly horrified.

'Oh, I don't know what made me say that! Steven, I'm so sorry.'

His face was shuttered and remote, so she looked at him earnestly and continued explaining.

'I do appreciate how much you've done for me, and how quickly you did it! I mean, I wanted to be here today. It's just that, well, I've been on my own for so long, that I found it strange when you arranged the day for both of us.'

She felt very relieved when he began to smile.

'All my girlfriends say I'm bossy,' he commented ruefully. 'I do tend to take over. I'll always negotiate,' he promised softly. 'All you have to do is tell me what you want, and I'll make sure that you get it.'

That queer breathlessness tightened in Araminta's chest again. She felt that they were somehow having two conversations at once. And she didn't like it. So she became businesslike.

'I must write to Fred Sparkle and thank him for giving me permission to enter his house,' she said quickly.

Steven leaned against his chair back and turned his attention to his coffee.

'It interested him. This is private, by the way. Fred doesn't mind publicity about the house, but his battle with his drinking problem is a different matter.'

'Of course.'

'Well, I don't know much about the treatment, but I gather it is pretty grim. Anyway, your romantic story gave him something to think about. Maybe he'll write a song about it.'

Araminta couldn't help feeling curious about such a famous person.

'Have you known him long?'

Steven offered her a shortcake biscuit. Their hands brushed lightly as Araminta took one. She moved away hastily as he answered.

'No. I've only met Fred twice. Once when he engaged me, and again to bring him up to date. I'm going to take him these measurements tomorrow, and then we'll decide what to do with the manor.'

Regretfully, Araminta decided that the coffee break had lasted long enough. She jumped down from the window seat and took up her brush. Then she turned back to Steven.

'I've started a record book, by the way. I'm saving a sample of all the carpets and curtains. That way it'll be easy to match the patterns when it comes to replacing them.'

Steven's eyes met hers squarely.

'That's very thoughtful of you, Araminta, but, I'm not sure that restoration is exactly what Fred Sparkle has in mind.'

Araminta felt cold.

'You mean he might modernise Thornclough Manor instead of restoring it? Is that why he turned down my offer to repair the glass panel?'

'I don't think he's decided what he's going to do yet,' Steven said calmly, but his eyes turned away as he said it.

Araminta picked up her broom.

'I'll keep the record anyway,' she said, fighting a sinking feeling in her stomach. 'It might be needed.'

'It might,' Steven said.

But there was a slight constraint between them that lasted until it was time for him to leave for Manchester.

'That's me finished. I'll be handing over to the architect from now on,' he told her.

Araminta couldn't tell how he felt about the prospect. If he was finished with Thornclough Manor, then they probably wouldn't meet again. The idea confused her. Her hands shook a little as she took the heavy, ornate key that Steven had had copied for her.

'Thank you for the key, and for getting me access and everything,' she said.

There was a lump in her throat that made talking difficult. She pushed a lock of hair back from her face, and then realised that the headscarf that she'd worn all day to keep her curls clean was slipping awry. She pulled it off absently and her curls tumbled down over her shoulders.

'Are you going to come here to search for your picture every day?' he asked her, his eyes lingering on hers.

'I'll try to come every day. I don't know how long I'll have access for, and of course, I'm eager to find it.'

There was a strained silence. Steven looked down and painted a pattern on the ground with the toe of his boot. It was a very solid brown boot, Araminta noted, that looked as if it had started life in the army.

'Good luck,' he said eventually, a little stiffly.

'Thank you,' Araminta said, equally stiffly.

'Right. I'll be going.'

He shot her a quick look under his lashes and looked away.

'Goodbye,' Araminta said.

'Goodbye,' Steven replied.

He turned, and Araminta watched his broad back as he walked out of the main door and down the three steps to the gravel below. Dusk was falling outside. Araminta dithered in the hallway. This was dreadful. He was going. But what could she do?

She heard the engine of the Range Rover spring to life. Then she heard it drive away, very quickly. Reacting rather than thinking, she ran out through the door and down the steps.

She could see two red tail-lights disappearing down the drive. Feeling desolate, she stood looking after them.

Then the lights stopped, and came back towards her as the Range Rover reversed rapidly, crunching over the gravel. Araminta felt a smile lifting her mouth upwards.

The door opened, and Steven jumped down from the driver's seat and came back to her. Drops of rain glinted in his hair, and Araminta thought again how clear and honest his grey eyes were.

'This is no good,' he said. 'Araminta, may I come and see you next weekend?'

'Oh, yes, please,' she said, the words tumbling out quickly. 'I'd like that.'

His smile was warm and jubilant.

'Friday night then?'

She couldn't help smiling back.

'Friday night,' she agreed.

6

Araminta had expected to feel nervous while she waited for Steven to show up on Friday night. All that week, their forthcoming meeting had been on her mind.

She had spent every daylight hour at Thornclough Manor, patiently sweeping up and looking in all the obvious places for her missing picture, to no avail. Whenever she thought of her approaching date, for this time, date it would most definitely be, she felt either pleasantly dreamy or unpleasantly tense, and sometimes both together.

But at the exact moment she heard Steven's knock on her cottage door, she hadn't given him a thought for hours. In fact she'd forgotten all about him.

Araminta rushed to the wooden stable door that led into her kitchen. In her haste, she opened only the top half of the door, and looked out at Steven over the bottom half.

'Hello,' she babbled nervously. 'It's lovely to see you, but I'm afraid that I'm not quite ready.'

Steven looked incredibly handsome and exactly right for a weekend in the country. He was wearing comfortable-looking silver-grey corduroy trousers and a cream Aran sweater that looked as if it had been knitted especially for him.

His eyebrows quirked upwards as he took in Araminta's grubby, ripped jeans and the milk that soaked the front of her tartan shirt.

'Hard day at the office?' he enquired sardonically.

'No, well, that is, yes, I mean . . . '

A gust of icy wind tugged at Araminta's hair and plastered her wet shirt to her front.

'Do come in,' she said hastily. 'You must be freezing out there.'

She had taken a few steps back into the kitchen before she realised that he wasn't following her. She repeated her invitation.

'Come in!'

Steven leaned over the bottom half of the stable door and grinned at her.

'It would help if you opened both halves of the door.'

'Oh, my goodness, yes. I'm so sorry.'

Feeling more frazzled than ever, Araminta hurried back and let him in. She was relieved that he came in laughing.

'There's no hurry,' he said, amusement lighting his grey eyes. 'I haven't booked a table anywhere, because we never got around to making any arrangements, but the Golden Lion say they can serve us any time tonight.'

Araminta smoothed back her hair.

'I was going to cook,' she said forlornly.

Steven's eyes followed hers across the stone-flagged floor to the pine kitchen table. It looked like the perfect illusion for a cookery book. Glowing in the circle of light from one of Araminta's glass lamp shades were the paper moons of white onions, luscious green peppers, finger-sized baby courgettes and a vibrantly red packet of best steak, all untouched as yet.

'Ah,' Steven said solemnly, 'bang go my hopes of home cooking.'

'I am sorry.'

Araminta began to apologise so earnestly, that Steven put his hand on her arm to stop her.

'I was teasing you,' he explained, his eyes glinting with amusement. 'It's obvious that something has cropped up. I've brought a bottle of wine. Let's have a drink and you can tell me all about it.'

Steven took the bottle opener from Araminta and opened the wine while she hunted for two glasses. Earlier on in the week, she had spring cleaned her little sitting-room and laid a real fire, but somehow, it seemed natural to settle at the kitchen table. Steven touched his glass lightly against hers.

'To a quiet life,' he said.

'A quiet life,' Araminta replied

fervently, lifting her glass. 'Oh, that tastes good.'

Exhausted, she leaned back in her seat for a minute and closed her eyes.

'You are the most extraordinary woman,' Steven said slowly.

Araminta kept her eyes closed. His smoky voice vibrated in her ears. She heard the deep rich velvety tones deepen as he continued.

'I've been trying to think what mysterious event could have made you completely forget our date, and in the process splatter you with what looks suspiciously like milk. You'll need to get that shirt off, by the way, and soak it. Have you been emergency baby-sitting?'

Araminta kept her eyes closed.

'You are so close to the mark,' she said softly. 'But what kind of baby?'

'A baby that's gone home, I hope,' he said, hiding his laughter.

Araminta shook her head.

'No, the baby, in fact, all four babies are still here.'

Steven's chair scraped as he leaned forward.

'Four babies!'

'Listen!' Araminta commanded softly. 'Can you hear them?'

She opened her eyes a slit, and, through her lashes, watched Steven cock his head, listening, scanning her pine kitchen for clues, homing in on a soft, contented noise at floor level.

'Squeaking!' he said triumphantly. 'In that cardboard box over by the cooker.'

'You got it,' Araminta said. 'Poor little things. Their mother was run over by a car. I think they have the hang of it now, but it took me an age to teach them about hand-feeding.'

'What are they, kittens?' Steven said, answering his own question and immediately asking another. 'Why didn't you take them to an animal sanctuary?'

'Because I haven't got transport, and I didn't want to call an inspector out. It's not really an emergency. I thought I'd see if I could get them to eat.' Araminta felt triumphant. 'And I did.'

'How often will you have to feed them?'

'Every four hours.'

'And as you've just fed them, you now have time to fit in a bath and dinner,' Steven said. 'Come on and I'll treat you to the best the Golden Lion has to offer.'

★   ★   ★

The squeaking from the cardboard box next to the cooker was both loud and desperate by the time Steven and Araminta returned from their long, leisurely, and most enjoyable meal at the Golden Lion.

'Poor babies! They are hungry,' she said, casting a guilty look at the clock. 'I'll light the fire and make you a drink, Steven. I bought a newspaper today, so you can relax in the sitting-room while I heat some milk.'

His mouth curved into a soft, amused smile.

'As if! You're not having all the fun.

Now where . . . Ah, I see it.'

He walked over to the space under the stone stairs that went to the top floor of the tiny cottage and opened the door of the battered fridge that sat there and took out a pink of milk.

'Glass bottles,' he remarked, 'and a Fifties' fridge. It's like stepping back in time.'

'I like it,' Araminta said, lifting the chrome lid of the stove and placing a saucepan on the hot plate.

'So do I.' Steven laughed. 'This cottage is just like you — full of surprises and unexpectedly attractive.'

Araminta tried to work out if that was a compliment or not as she poured milk into the saucepan, but before she'd come to a conclusion, Steven distracted her by asking, 'Did your grandfather's bequest to his tenants include you?'

'Sadly not. I'm sub-letting this house, so I didn't qualify.'

'That's a shame,' Steven said.

He had managed to unearth the

plastic droppers Araminta had borrowed to feed her orphans with.

'These are tiny. Do they need sterilising?'

'There's a bottle of solution on the sink,' she replied, thinking how handy he was, and how nice it was to have someone to help her.

She watched as he read the instructions on the bottle, mixed the solution and sterilised the equipment. His task complete, Steven gave her a serious look.

'It's a shame you didn't inherit your cottage at least,' he said, 'especially since there's no sign of your picture as yet.'

'I know.' Araminta sighed. 'But I'm still looking.'

Steven's eyes were warm and concerned.

'Did you meet the architect? I warned her to expect to find you raking about in the house.'

'No, no-one's been to the house while I've been there.'

'Perhaps she'll start next week. I know Fred Sparkle has asked her to schedule it as a rush job. He wants the house ready to move into at the end of his treatment.'

Araminta felt a cold block in her stomach.

'When will that be?'

Steven shook his head.

'I'm not sure exactly. It could be months.'

But Araminta's feeling of relief was short-lived, because he went on.

'That is to say, a job the size of Thornclough Manor would usually take months. Fred may be planning to hire extra builders and rush the job through. I wouldn't know about it anymore. My part of the job is finished now that the architect has taken over.'

Araminta swung round to face him, feeling dismayed.

'Then you won't have to come to Thornclough again?'

His eyes were very dark and intent as they met hers.

'I didn't have to come down here this weekend. I came to see you, Araminta.'

His face was very close to hers. She felt her mouth go dry as he put out one gentle hand and touched her hair very, very lightly. She drew in a sharp breath and her hand flew up to catch his.

He stopped moving, but he kept his hand where it was, maintaining the contact between them. His disarming grey eyes looked into Araminta's brown ones. She scanned his face urgently, trying to read his intentions, trying to fathom his soul.

Steven waited patiently. A slight upwards curve to his lips suggested that he was confident that she would come to him. And then they were both startled by a violent hissing noise beside them. The cloying smell of burned milk filled the air, and drops of liquid ran hissing over the surface of the stove.

It was a relief to turn away, but under the flurry of clearing up the mess and putting the salvaged milk on the windowsill to cool, Araminta's heart was beating wildly. Did she want him to kiss her or not?

She thought that, on the whole, maybe she did. On the other hand, she had never been so frightened of a man in her life, which was ridiculous. She had nothing to be afraid of. Look how careful he'd been to book a room at the Golden Lion, putting her under no pressure. Look how quickly he'd backed off when she'd put her hand up. He was the perfect gentleman. And yet . . . And yet . . .

And yet he could hurt me, Araminta admitted. I like him so much that he could hurt me. That's what scares me. We come from such different worlds. How long is he going to spend in a tiny village with little Miss Country Mouse? And how will I feel when he gets tired of me?

As if he had been reading her mind, Steven returned to a subject they had discussed over dinner.

'I am sorry that I have to get back in the morning. It would have been nice to help you hunt for your picture tomorrow, and on Sunday, too, come to that.'

'I should open my shop on Sunday. I had several indignant phone calls during the week, asking why it was closed last Sunday. I'm just about managing to keep up with my commissions by working at night while I search the house all day.' Araminta sighed. 'I'd like to spend every day searching for my picture, but I can't afford to lose any business by shutting the workshop.'

'Well, I could have helped you with the shop, whatever you were doing.' Steven's eyes were warm. 'I was just looking forward to a weekend in the country, but business has cropped up, I'm afraid. Prince Farsid insisted and I don't like to let him down.'

Araminta suppressed a faint regret. It would have been nice to spend the weekend with Steven.

'Well, of course you must go if he needs you. He sounds like a good friend to have. You say he steers a lot of business your way.'

Steven smiled at her gratefully and touched her hand lightly.

'Thank you for being so reasonable, sweetheart. I shall miss being with you, but I have to say that the prince's prize sounds intriguing.'

Araminta shook her head.

'How the other half lives. What, exactly, does he want you to do?'

'He has his eye on selling some old warehouses. I should imagine it will be a simple case of valuation and a quick sale. The funny thing is that I just happen to know a company that's looking for that kind of industrial property. New York style loft conversions are all the thing at the moment.'

'Not my thing,' Araminta muttered, but she was distracted by a fresh outburst of squalling from the cardboard box.

'Hold on, babies,' she called. 'The milk should be cool enough now.'

She was aware of Steven watching her as she retrieved the saucepan and filled one of the very small eyedroppers.

'Perfect,' she decided, testing a drop on the inside of her wrist.

'I'll help you feed them,' Steven insisted, taking another of the tiny feeders.

But when Araminta lifted the cardboard box on the pine table and offered Steven one of the piteously squeaking bundles, he backed off smartly, looking aghast.

'What, in the name of all that's wonderful, is that?'

Araminta looked down at the unlovely pink bundle she held. It was warm and pulsated in her hand. She looked up at Steven.

'It's a hedgehog,' she informed him.

'A hedgehog?'

Steven peered at the wriggling baby.

'It's the ugliest thing I've ever seen in my life,' he pronounced. 'And if it's a hedgehog, where are its spiky things?'

Araminta stifled a giggle.

'They aren't born with spines.' She

laughed. 'Think of the poor mothers!'

She stroked the rubbery white spines that bristled out of the pink baby body.

'These will fill out, darken, and become spines as the baby gets older, which it won't, if I don't get some milk into it.'

Steven's mouth quirked downwards in disgust.

'I was expecting cute, fluffy kittens,' he complained.

But he brushed off Araminta's suggestion that he retreat to the sitting-room with the newspaper. Instead, he firmly took hold of one ugly orphan.

'Come to Uncle Steven then,' he said resignedly.

And he didn't even seem to mind when he had to teach it all over again just what the eyedropper was for. When the second baby had finally been coaxed into drinking, Steven looked over at Araminta with a smile in his eyes.

'Have you named them yet?' he asked kindly.

'I haven't had time to think of names yet.'

'It's probably better to wait until their personalities develop,' Steven remarked, looking down at the scrawny pink baby in his hand, 'although this one is much bigger than the others, and bolder, too. I think he looks like a Norman. Storming Norman, the hedgehog commando.'

'Norman he shall be.' Araminta laughed. 'Or possibly Norma. I have no idea how one sexes a hedgehog.'

'Talking of names, your is both charming and unusual, Araminta. Is it a family name?'

'Very much so. My mother was an Araminta, and so was her mother. In fact, if you look in the churchyard you'll see that it's full of Aramintas. The first one goes back to the seventeenth century.'

'The churchyard here? At Thorn-clough?'

'Yes. There have been Araminta Shaws in Thornclough for hundreds of years.'

'I'm confused. Was your father a Shaw, too?'

Araminta laughed.

'No. He was a Boutsikaris, Alexander Boutsikaris. He decided that, as he was living in England, he would take an English name, my mother's. That's why I'm a Shaw instead of a Boutsikaris.'

'It suits you,' Steven said, smiling at her. 'Or at least, the name Araminta suits you when you are being grave and grown-up and old-fashioned, but a lot of the time you are like a little girl, bubbling over with fun and mischief. Would you mind if I called you Minty sometimes?'

She smiled at him and then had to swallow and look away.

'That's what my parents called me, when we were laughing and joking.'

His glance was a sympathetic caress.

'You miss them still.'

'Oh, yes, especially my mother. I was

ten when my father died, so I've kind of had time to get used to that. But mother . . . '

Araminta felt tears sting her eyes.

'Down you go, Norman,' Steven said.

Ignoring the pleading squeaks, he placed the infant firmly, but gently, in its box. Then he swiftly closed the space between himself and Araminta. His sweater was warm and comforting and Araminta nuzzled into it as if she were a puppy. His arms went around her as if they belonged there. His hands were gentle as they stroked her head.

He stood patiently holding her as she sobbed. The storm of emotion, although sharp, was brief. She soon regained her control, sniffing and wiping her eyes, tilting her head back to look up at him through the starburst of tears.

'I'm sorry.'

There was warmth and strength in the way his arms held her close.

'Don't apologise for feeling, Minty, darling.'

He pulled away a little so that he could look at her with tender eyes.

'You cry, and laugh, and, yes, blush, too, with all the unaffected charm and spontaneity of a child. It's one of the things I like best about you.'

Araminta sniffed.

'You like me?'

It seemed hard to believe that such a sophisticated man could be attracted by her, but he was smiling down at her with a world of affection in his expression.

'I just called you darling,' he pointed out gravely.

Joy filled Araminta's heart. A smile tugged the corners of her lips upwards.

'So you did,' she remembered. 'Darling Minty, that's what you said.'

His agreement was soft.

'That's what I said.'

Steven inclined his head towards her, holding her close to him. This time Araminta did not pull away. She stood happily within the circle of his arms. They stood in silence for a few moments, just savouring the closeness. She closed her eyes for a moment and leaned into the strength of Steven's body. He smelled of the outdoors with a faint tang of aftershave.

Steven put one gentle hand on her chin and tipped her face up so that their eyes met.

'I called you darling because you are a darling,' he whispered softly. 'The very nicest darling I know.'

And he touched her lips gently with his.

Araminta melted into the kiss with a soft, happy sigh. She felt at home. She felt as if all the lonely places in her heart had been filled. She felt, no she knew, that nothing had ever been as right as this kiss. Steven raised his head and hugged her to him softly.

'My darling,' he said with great tenderness and decision. 'I could kiss you all night. But, I have just seen the clock, and tongues will be wagging if I do not present myself before the doors of the Golden Lion are locked.'

He planted a gentle, and rueful, kiss in the centre of Araminta's forehead.

'I wish I didn't have to get back, but I do. I wish I didn't have to leave early in the morning, but I do.'

He looked at her with smiling eyes and shook his head.

'So many wishes!'

Greatly daring, Araminta stood on her tiptoes to press a kiss on his mouth.

'I have wishes, too,' she murmured. 'I wish that you would come again next weekend.'

His smile was warm.

'Do you want me to?'

She laughed and nuzzled into him.

'Can't you tell?'

A look of feigned puzzlement and a shake of the head.

'I can't be sure.'

She couldn't resist hugging him and kissing him again. Then she breathed the words earnestly, 'I want you to come and see me next weekend.'

Steven threw his head back. There

was a joyous, almost triumphant ring to his laugh.

'Then I want to come. I will come. Will Friday night suit you?'

Their eyes met in a wordless promise. Araminta's heart was beating wildly, but she pressed on.

'You can stay with me, if you like. It's silly to keep paying pub prices. I have a sofa bed.'

His hug was warm and reassuring.

'I shall be happy to sleep on your sofa bed,' he said, looking at her gravely, letting her know that he understood her feelings and respected them.

Then he bent his head to brush her lips with his once more. His kiss was loving, giving and patient, and Araminta knew it was going to be all right.

7

Two weeks later, early on Friday evening, Araminta was listening with all her ears for the sound of Steven's Range Rover arriving at her cottage as she scooted around the kitchen. She was nearly ready for him. Dinner was in the oven and the baby hedgehogs had been fed. There was just the washing up to do, and the sitting-room fire to lay.

Bother! Her thoughts broke off with a snap. She'd forgotten to chop the logs! And there was the distinctive sound of a six-cylinder engine, pulling up outside. As the car door slammed, she gave up the unequal battle with the housekeeping and pulled off her apron, smoothing her hair down with both hands as she ran for the door.

On the other side of the door, Steven was running to meet her. Despite the light spring rain that was falling,

Araminta had left the top half of the stable door open while she was cooking. Now she leaned over one side of the wooden door and Steven leaned over the other, and their lips met in a long, lingering kiss.

'Oh, I missed you!' Steven said finally, tearing himself away. 'Let's get this door open, then I can hold you in my arms.'

Araminta opened the bottom half of the door for him, and he came into the kitchen, laughing, his arms full of goodies. A lavish bunch of flowers seriously impeded his view. Just visible amongst the foliage was a brown grocery sack from an Italian delicatessen which smelled deliciously of coffee. Araminta could see the neck of a bottle of wine poking out between two crusty loaves of bread. A smaller carrier bag dangling from one finger proclaimed that he had stopped at a speciality chocolate store.

'For you, darling,' he said, thrusting the flowers at her and dumping the food on the table. 'Come here and let me hug you.'

'You'll crush them!' Araminta protested, whisking her flowers out of harm's way.

Steven pursued her laughingly, but she fended him off until the flowers were up to their necks in a bucket of water.

'I don't get flowers often enough to let them get crushed,' she said, straightening up and holding out her arms for Steven.

He swept her up and wrapped her tightly in his arms.

'I'll buy you flowers every day,' he promised extravagantly, kissing her forehead. 'I want you to have everything you want.'

'I've got everything I want,' she said softly, 'right here in my arms.'

And there was silence in the warm kitchen as the two lovers made up for a whole week of separation. Steven eventually managed to tear himself away.

'Oh, my,' he said, breathing rather quickly, 'if I could bottle your kisses, I'd be a millionaire. But come here, let me look at you. How has your week been? Talking on the phone just isn't enough for me. I want you to start again and tell me your news over. Has anything happened?'

'No, why?'

Araminta stared at him, puzzled.

He moved her gently into the circle of brighter light cast by the pendant light that hung over the kitchen table. He pulled it down so that the glow fell on her face.

'Because you look exhausted, that's why. The hollows in your cheeks are too deep and there are violet shadows under your eyes.'

Touched by the concern in his eyes, Araminta was nevertheless quick to deny that there was anything wrong.

'I'm fine,' she lied.

Steven looked unconvinced, but he didn't press her.

'Maybe what we both need is dinner

and an early night,' he said gently. 'I must confess that I'm tired myself. It's been a busy week, but profitable, so I shouldn't grumble.'

Araminta began bustling around the kitchen.

'I've made a casserole,' she gabbled. 'I'll just wash a few plates and open the wine and look out some glasses.'

'Stop!'

Steven was laughing, but his eyes were serious.

'You don't have to rush around after me, Araminta. Let me help. If you've gone to all the trouble of cooking a meal, the least I can do is set the table and dish it out.'

'Thank you, but it's easier if I do it,' she said. 'But I tell you what we do need if we want a fire tonight — logs.'

'Logs?' Steven echoed, looking a bit put out.

Then he gave a shrug that visibly put to one side his feelings of tiredness and hunger.

'Sure, I'll go get them. But will your

supplier still be open?'

Araminta chuckled.

'Here's my supplier,' she said, holding out a sharp axe. 'There's a pile of logs in my workshop. I keep my firewood there because it's nice and dry.'

'You chop your own logs?'

'Logs, packing crates, left-over builder's wood. If it's cheap, I'll burn it.'

Steven looked at her directly, his mouth in a grim line.

'You shouldn't be using a heavy axe like this. For heaven's sake, Araminta, why don't you get an electric fire?'

She turned away from him, her heart feeling sore at the criticism.

'I can assure you that I'm quite capable of using an axe,' she told him stiffly. 'I'm no fragile flower.'

'I'm sorry,' Steven said at once, and his tone echoed the sincerity in his eyes. 'I didn't mean that in a sexist way. Remember, I've got a mother who used to drive a tank! No, I was thinking about the work, and the inconvenience for you. It's like living in the dark ages. Fancy having to chop wood every time you want a fire. My place has gas central heating. One touch of the button is all it takes.'

'Well, my place doesn't,' Araminta said firmly. 'So it's chop logs or freeze.'

She looked at Steven more happily. His frank apology had made her feel better. She held out her hand.

'Give me the axe. I'll do it.'

He lifted the axe away from her.

'No, no. I'll do it. Is there a log basket?'

'Two,' Araminta said. 'One in the bedroom and one in the sitting-room.'

Araminta heard Steven's feet thudding overhead as he ran upstairs for the basket. She smiled as she took the heavy kettle off the stove. She supposed her cottage was inconvenient, but it was cheap and she loved it, and you soon got used to it. And to modernise it in any way would cost quite a bit.

She felt the chill that always assailed her when the gulf that lay between her life and Steven's was brought to her attention. He lived in a world where you pushed a button and the work was done for you, a world where a few pounds could solve any problem. She could feel him looking at her when he rejoined her in the kitchen.

'You give yourself so much work,' he said as he deposited the logs. 'And I notice your hot water supply is faulty. It's that old stove. I'll get it fixed for you.'

Araminta was furious.

'It's ridiculous to spend money on the landlord's property,' she snapped.

'But you have to live in it,' Steven pointed out reasonably.

'And I like it the way it is!' she replied, horrified to hear a suspicion of tears in her voice.

Suddenly she wanted him to go away and leave her alone. How dare he barge into her quiet life and start criticising the way she did things?

'I like it just the way it is. Why have you suddenly started pulling my house to shreds? You never complained about it last week.'

Steven's deep chuckle was soothing. He pulled her into his arms.

'Darling Minty,' he said, pushing her hair out of her eyes with one tender hand, 'last week I was in such a delightful haze that I could have been on the moon and never noticed a thing. All I noticed was you. All I could think about was you.'

His kiss was very tender. He bent his head to look at her earnestly.

'And I'm still thinking about you. If I'm complaining, it's only because I want things to be easier for you, that's all.'

Araminta let herself be soothed. She let her head rest on his broad chest.

'I'm sorry,' she said. 'I'm tired.'

'We both are, and hungry. Let me help you. What do you say we eat in the kitchen and then take a bottle of wine to the sitting-room? I've chopped enough logs for one fire.'

Araminta looked up at him smiling.

Later, as they sat in front of the roaring fire watching the firelight flicker on the walls, Steven turned serious. He smoothed Araminta's tangled hair back from her forehead.

'I'm worried about you, Minty,' he said softly.

She turned her head up to look at him and gave him a sleepy smile.

'Worried? Whatever is there to worry about?'

He didn't reply immediately, so Araminta relaxed. His hands felt nice stroking her hair. The wind seemed to have got stronger. It stirred the gaily-patterned chintz curtains and rain tapped against the window.

'Isn't it funny,' she said dreamily, 'how bad weather outside makes being inside seem more cosy?'

Steven shifted his weight slightly and smiled.

'It certainly is cosy in here, despite the somewhat Spartan conditions, but don't change the subject, Minty! I'm worried about you because you are running yourself ragged. How many hours sleep are you getting every night?'

Araminta lifted her head again to consider him. There was something about the gravity of his expression that made her decide against lying to him. She settled for a gentle evasion.

'Plenty,' she said, trying to inject conviction into her tone. 'I don't need a lot of sleep, anyway.'

Steven bent his head and dropped a gentle kiss on her nose.

'The army knows a lot about getting the utmost out a person,' he remarked.

Araminta stared at him, puzzled.

'Excuse me?'

His eyes were loving, but there was determination in them, too. He wanted her to understand what he meant.

'Anyone can make a supreme effort for a short time, but if you keep it up, if you run at full throttle for too long, you'll burn out and crash. You mustn't go on like this. I suspect that you are spending every daylight hour combing Thornclough Manor for your picture, sitting up late at night to carry out your normal work, and then getting up every four hours to feed those damned orphans of yours. Am I right?'

Araminta felt guilty, but she answered him honestly.

'I suppose so.'

'Darling, you can't carry on at this rate. You must pace yourself, take a rest, shed a few unimportant tasks. Why not let me take the hedgehogs to an animal sanctuary?'

'No! They came to me, and they are doing so well with me. They know me now and they take food so easily. Every day they get stronger. And when they are a bit bigger, I'll introduce them to my garden and they can run free in their own area. You know the nest was in the ditch right opposite my house. This is where they belong.'

There was a definite note of exasperation in Steven's voice now.

'Are you telling me that those hedgehogs would care where they lived? Hedgehogs don't get sentimental over birthplaces! You are projecting human emotions on to them, Minty.'

She felt convinced that she was right, but, regarding the obstinate line of Steven's jaw, she prudently switched the line of her argument to more practical issues.

'I'm also worried about infection. The babies are so healthy here. There are no other animals to bring in possible diseases. Who knows what they'd pick up?'

She felt Steven's body move in exasperation.

'I'm sure the sanctuary takes all possible precautions.'

And then she remembered a horrid fact. She was amazed that it had slipped her mind for even a few hours, but in the pleasure of having Steven with her for the weekend, it had gone away until this moment. She sat bolt up right.

'But it doesn't matter,' she said urgently. 'It's just as you said, a short-term situation. Everything's going to change.'

Steven caught the seriousness of her tone. Araminta was struck again by his air of authority. She found it very comforting, but she gave a little sigh. Not even Steven would be able to help her with this.

'The builders start work on Monday,' she said miserably, 'and I have to stop my search when they move in. The site manager was very sympathetic, but it's a matter of insurance. Once his firm moves in, they are responsible for all health and safety matters. The firm's policy won't allow a non-employee on the premises while work is in progress.'

Steven's eyes were sympathetic.

'What if you had your own insurance?' he suggested.

'What if I could pay for it.' Araminta sighed. 'We rang the builder's insurers, but the sum they quoted was just laughable.'

Steven's hand touched hers sympathetically, but she couldn't help just a tinge of crossness in her voice and she tossed her curls back over her shoulder.

'So you see, Steven, all your concern for me was misplaced. I'm not going to burn out, because, after this weekend, life will be back to normal. I knew what I was doing.'

'Ouch!' He grinned. 'You are like a little wild cat caught in a trap, all fizz and scratches if anyone tries to help you. If I offended, I'm sorry, but you're just going to have to get used to accepting concern for your well-being from another human being, and a man at that. I'll never be able to see you wearing yourself out without trying to help you.'

Araminta regarded him cautiously while a mixed torrent of feelings ripped through her. He sounded as if he intended to be around for a while, but on the other hand, she doubted the wisdom of relaxing her control and allowing herself to lean on a man who would surely leave her for life in the city as soon as he got fed up with the novelty of roughing it out in the countryside. It was better, far better to be independent. That way you couldn't get hurt.

'I appreciate what you're saying,' she replied finally, thinking even as she spoke how handsome he looked. 'But I can look after myself.'

Steven's eyes glinted at her wickedly and he reached out his arms and drew her close.

'Oh, what a shame,' he teased. 'Thinking I'd be spending all weekend helping you root around in old attics and cellars looking for your picture, I brought some dreadful old clothes with me, and now you won't get the pleasure of seeing them. I'll just have to pack them away and slink off back to the city.'

Araminta regarded him anxiously.

'You don't have to go home,' she protested. 'If it's nice you could read the newspaper in the garden. I'll make lunch.'

'What is it with this girl?' he demanded of the crackling log fire. 'She keeps shoving me off to read the paper while she has fun with hedgehogs and old houses. She's just selfish. She just doesn't like sharing.'

'I don't!' Araminta squealed. 'I mean I do!'

'I'll be off then, seeing as I'm not wanted.'

Even in jest, it was hard to say the words.

'You are wanted,' Araminta said, and she felt as if Steven could see how serious she was and that she'd made a huge, and possibly dangerous admittance.

'So?' he finally demanded, 'do you want my help or not?'

'I do want your help tomorrow.'

'Good,' he murmured huskily, his voice growing deep and serious as his kisses deepened. 'Then it's upstairs to bed for you. I'll see you in the morning. It looks as if we are both going to have a busy day tomorrow.'

8

No matter how slowly and carefully Araminta pushed at her sitting-room door, she couldn't stop it creaking. Giving up the attempt to creep in, she flung the door wide and marched in with the breakfast tray.

'Wake up, lazy bones,' she cried gaily, putting the tray down on the coffee table for a moment and opening the curtains. 'There's an incredible dawn sky outside.'

Despite the wonderful flush that coloured the morning, Steven rolled over in the sofa bed with a groan and put his pillow over his head, jamming it down hard over his ears.

'Wake up? I haven't been able to sleep at all!' he grumbled.

'Why didn't you sleep?' she enquired.

'I can't believe you can't hear the wretched things. Cockerels! They've been sounding off since three o'clock this morning. I've never heard a row like it.'

A deep crease appeared between his brows.

'What's so funny?'

Araminta stifled a giggle.

'I'm sorry, but you get used to them, living in the country. Now that I listen I can hear them,' she admitted. 'But I quite like the sound, and you surely can't dislike the other birds? I wouldn't like to start the day without a bit of bird song.'

'A man needs a bit of peace in the morning,' he grumbled.

'Trucks,' she remarked. 'Garbage trucks, delivery trucks, and then rush-hour traffic; horns and engines and squealing brakes. You can't tell me it's quiet in the middle of Manchester first thing in the morning.'

'I've got double glazing,' Steven said grumpily. But he looked more cheerful as he sniffed the air. 'That coffee smells good,' he admitted.

'Have some toast,' she offered, passing him a hot plate and then a slice of well-buttered brown toast.

'More!' Steven demanded a few minutes later. 'This is the best toast I've ever eaten in my life! What delicious bread, and the marmalade is just perfect. Where do you get it?'

'I made them,' Araminta said, smiling sunnily at the compliments. 'I'll give you some marmalade to take home. I've got plenty because I was lucky at the market last Saturday afternoon — a whole box of the best marmalade oranges for practically nothing.'

Steven was staring at her in total disbelief.

'You're mad! You're stark, staring mad!' he exploded, indignation darkening his eyes. 'As if running your career, bringing up four babies and hunting for your heirloom weren't enough, you have to make marmalade, and bread! What on earth do you think you're playing at? What are shops for if not to make your life easier?'

Araminta glared back at him.

'How I run my life is my affair,' she pointed out icily.

Instantly Steven put his toast and coffee aside to reach for her.

'I'm sorry,' he said, his tone gentle. 'I've put my foot in it again. I'm not criticising you, but the amount of work you do. Minty, darling, I want things to be better for you.'

'Things are just fine,' she snapped.

He held her tight.

'No, they are not. You are carrying much too heavy a burden. Listen!' he continued. 'I want you to come home with me on Monday morning. Come back to my Manchester flat, spend the week with me. You'll see how easy life can be in a nice, modern place.'

Araminta felt like a snail being prised out of its shell. Much as she liked Steven, she didn't want to leave home.

'There's the hedgehogs,' she mumbled, 'and my work, the picture . . . '

'We'll find a baby-sitter for your orphans,' Steven insisted. 'And I'll introduce you to some art dealers I know. One in particular could help you a great deal, so you could call it a business trip. And as for your picture, darling, we have to face facts. If it hasn't been found by Monday morning, then it never will be. It would be better for you to come to Manchester with me than to sit at home brooding about it.'

While Araminta was thinking about it, he held her close and looked at her with such affection that she had almost made up her mind to say yes even before he touched her cheek with a gentle hand and said softly, 'Please come. I want the chance to look after you and spoil you. You'll see how happy I can make you.'

Against her better judgement, Araminta allowed herself to be persuaded.

'Are you sure you want me?' she asked in a small voice. 'There seems to be a lot about me that you criticise.'

'Criticise you? Never!' he assured her. 'I've never met a woman I've felt less like criticising. You're perfect just as you are.'

Pacified, Araminta reached for another piece of toast.

'And I do make good toast, admit it,' she demanded, a teasing light in her eyes.

'This is the best breakfast I've ever had in my life,' Steven declared with perfect sincerity. 'The best toast, the best marmalade, the best coffee.'

He paused and looked at her with a soft expression and added in a lower voice, 'And the best company a man could have. No wonder I feel so happy, so alive! I feel as if today's going to be special. Let's get out of here. Maybe today will be the day we find your picture.'

★   ★   ★

The muffled explosion was followed by a cloud of evil-smelling smoke and a shower of sparks that set Araminta's heart racing. What if she'd broken

Steven's microwave oven?

The shrill, urgent clamour of the kitchen smoke alarm added to the chaos. Araminta dived for the power supply at the wall and turned it off. Once the oven was safe, she jumped up on to the shiny work surface of the kitchen units and reached up to deal with the smoke alarm. Then she scrambled back down to gaze in trepidation at the closed door of the now silent microwave.

She'd followed Steven's instructions implicitly. He'd told her to call at the supermarket for a hot, ready-roasted chicken and some prepared salads for dinner that evening. All she had to do, he said, was to pop the chicken in the microwave two minutes before he was due home.

Araminta cautiously opened the microwave door. Smoke billowed out. The paper bag that held the chicken was charred and smouldering. Using a tea towel to protect her hands, she lifted out the whole sorry mess and carried it to the sink that gleamed below the window. She dumped the bag in the sink and poked around the blackened disaster.

The paper bag had been lined with foil. Araminta had a dim recollection of hearing that one could not put metal in a microwave. Perhaps that had been the problem. There was no way of finding out.

Steven had said that she wouldn't need an instruction book. All she had to do was pop the food in the oven and push the button, he had said, smiling. It would be so easy she would wonder how she had lived without the help of modern technology.

Araminta studied the control panel of the cooker. It was covered with unhelpful symbols and flashing lights. She shook her head sadly. It was beyond her. She went back to the chicken and removed it from the ruined packaging. She studied it gravely. It didn't look damaged. She put it on a plate. Then she cleared away the debris.

It took a long time to locate every charred flake of paper, which had drifted all over the kitchen.

When all the kitchen surfaces were restored to their chilly level of hospital hygiene, she went back to the chicken and examined it gloomily. It looked OK. She wondered if it would still be possible to eat that chicken and enjoy it, after the disaster!

Araminta sighed. She thought perhaps not. Quite apart from the possibility that it had picked up the flavour of the smoke, it had never been a very attractive chicken in the first place. It was a burned khaki colour that she found most off-putting, and, because someone had extracted the bones and then sewed the carcass up again, it was a very peculiar shape.

The ready-made salads, as well, looked somewhat the worse for wear. Somehow they had turned themselves upside down in her bag on the way home. They must have got shaken, too. They had coagulated into solid lumps and gone rather oily. If there had been any fresh salad around, Araminta would have tried to dress it up a bit, but Steven's bare, clinical kitchen held nothing that she recognised as food at all, so she was forced to put the battered salads out on a plate and just leave them.

Shrugging, Araminta got herself a glass of icy, sparkling mineral water and wandered through into the vastness of the lounge to wait for Steven. If she tried to rush out to the shops now, she would probably miss him. Better wait until he came home. She would confess her misadventures and they would decide what was best to do. Idly, she wandered over to one of the windows and stood by the cool glass, looking out at the rainswept day.

The one thing Araminta liked about Steven's apartment was the panoramic view. Most of the walls were made of specially-glazed plate glass, and she could see for miles over the centre of Manchester. Evening was falling. The sky, which had been steel-grey all day, was turning a suffused navy blue. A grey train, small as a child's toy from this height, ran smoothly into the station.

But Araminta now saw that the cars were strings of unmoving headlights in the jammed streets below. The stalled traffic was doubtless the explanation for Steven's lateness. Araminta was glad he hadn't come home on time and found her racing around the kitchen, but now she wished he was back. Perhaps when Steven arrived, some of her unhappiness would dissipate.

Slowly, she turned away from the window and wandered over to the white leather sofa. The plastic of the light birchwood-effect floor was cold on her bare feet so she tucked them up under her. The leather skin of the sofa was cold beneath her and she longed for the comfortable warmth of her tatty old blanket-covered sofa at home.

She looked round the glossy apartment and sighed. She picked up a brochure that lay on the glass coffee table and flicked through the glossy pages. It was advertising yet more loft-style apartments in the old industrial areas of Manchester. She looked at the name on the back cover.

It had been put out by the company that had bought the warehouses from Prince Farsid. She knew that Steven had been happy to sell the prince's property to them. He genuinely admired the company's beautifully-crafted conversions. Indeed, he had bought his own apartment from them.

She turned over a few more pages of the brochure, trying to appreciate the style by learning more about it. Some of the photographs made the rooms look beautiful in a bare, stylistic Japanese manner, but to Araminta the properties just didn't look homely. She dropped the brochure back on the glass table and looked around Steven's austere apartment again.

The refurbishment had been beautifully done, and no expense had been spared. Steven's white leather suite alone must have cost more than every single piece of furniture Araminta had ever owned, and probably all her clothes and artist's tools into the bargain, but she didn't care. She hated it. It was cold, bare and uncomfortable. She wanted to go home.

But going home would mean leaving Steven, and he was the nicest man she had ever met and she knew that she was well on the way to being in love with him. She leaned forward for her drink, hating the way the leather creaked as she moved. She took a sip of her water and felt the bubbles fizzing on her tongue. Who was she kidding? She was already totally, irrevocably in love with Steven.

But could you love the man and not his lifestyle, Araminta wondered. Her thoughts went back to the argument of the previous day. Steven had insisted on spending all Sunday in her workshop with her. Like most things to do with Steven, it had been a mixed delight.

It was lovely to have his company all day; lovely to see him proudly showing off her work to prospective customers; lovely, as she was busy piecing together delicately-coloured bits of glass, to look up from her soldering iron and see him comfortably installed in her scruffy armchair in front of the paraffin stove, head bent over the Sunday papers.

It was nice, too, to have him bring her coffee and insist on treating her to lunch. He had even held the fort while she rushed home to feed the hedge-hogs. All those things had been wonderful. He had, on the other hand, hurt her feelings dreadfully.

Compared to most of the other artists Araminta had met throughout her life, she was comfortably aware that she was a marvel of organisation. Her workshop was spotless, her commissions always executed on time, and her cash flow, although more a cash trickle, was so organised that her bills were all paid by the due date. It was something she felt rather proud of, for she knew that few other artists, her father included, were so organised.

And then Steven came along telling her that she was missing golden business opportunities! His criticism hurt dreadfully, but Araminta was honest enough to wonder if he could possibly be right. He had suggested that she mass produce some of her smaller pieces, such as the gay scarab beetles that were designed to fly in people's windows, both catching the light and bringing them luck.

When Araminta had protested that she was proud that each piece was individually crafted, Steven had asked her if she was sure that was of major interest to the customers. He had gone on to point out that she could perhaps change the design every month, and that if she then varied the colour schemes slightly, each piece would still be very different.

When she had rebuffed his sugges-tion by saying that she didn't want to be a production line, he had taken her breath away by calmly suggesting that she take on an apprentice. A young person would carry out much of the repetitive work in exchange for the chance to learn the trade from a real, practising artist. And when Araminta said that she had never considered employing anyone and that she couldn't afford the wages, he had accused her of being too lazy to look into government subsidies.

Steven had only pointed out all the advantages of such a scheme for both parties involved, but also had turned all her ideas upside down by suggesting that it was her duty to take on a young person and help give them a start in life. Could he be right?

Four hours since their last meal! Araminta glanced at her watch now and half rose in alarm, before laughing at herself and sinking back on the sofa. The hedgehog orphans had become so much a part of her life that it felt very strange not to be feeding them every four hours. That duty had been passed on to a very willing Mrs Ishak.

Steven, on one of his trips to the village shop for supplies, had somehow managed to persuade, or possibly bribe, the postmistress into assuming the care and feeding of four round, fat, cyclamen-pink baby hedgehogs, so that Araminta would be free to accompany him to Manchester.

A feeling of homesickness engulfed Araminta as she thought of the village shop. She supposed in time one would get to know all the faces at the huge supermarket around the corner, but could that ever be the same? A reminiscent smile tugged her lips as she remembered sitting in the back row of the village hall with Mrs Ishak last month.

The postmistress had clung to Araminta in a frenzy of stage fright on behalf of her child, but her youngest had performed his part in the concert as if he were a seasoned actor. He remembered every single action, and all the words, as did his classmates.

The mothers relaxed. The school concert had been declared a resounding success.

She and Steven had been to the theatre last night to see a modern play. Araminta shuddered at the thought. By the end of the evening she still had no idea what the play was about, although the actors had shouted a lot. The whole thing had struck her as a complete waste of time. It was small comfort to remember that Steven had cheerfully admitted that it had baffled him, too. It made her realise how little she knew him. Why had he bought tickets for such an obscure play? Would he often expect her to go to events like that? She shivered again, but this time she realised that the sensation was physical.

It was cold in the apartment, as it had been all the long, lonely day. Araminta got up and had another look at the state-of-the-art thermostat. She turned it up again. The flashing numbers were trying to tell her that the temperature in the room was quite high, but somehow Araminta just couldn't get warm.

She walked over to the window and checked the traffic again. It was moving so slowly that it almost looked still. Tiny blue and yellow flashing lights showed where the police and emergency services were trying to move the obstruction — an oil tanker lying on its side. Araminta hoped Steven would be home soon.

Of course, she was not used to spending an idle day. Time would not hang so heavily once she had a workshop established nearby. Steven had been most helpful about that, as he had about everything. He said that he had made the perfect arrangement for her. The very next day she had an appointment with a Mr Tamworth, who owned a big gallery in the centre of Manchester. He helped artists to find studio space in cheaper areas of the city, and, in return, sold their works in his central gallery.

Steven had been a bit vague about

the exact terms of the arrangement, but Araminta hoped it would work. She hoped everything would work. She knew that Steven was doing everything he could to help her get used to his lifestyle, efforts he had never made for another woman. She was the first female who'd ever been invited to share his life. He was making a huge effort to adjust. And she was grateful, she was. It was just that . . .

A click at the door made her leap up. She was running for the door as soon as she was sure that it was his key in the lock. The door opened. Steven came in laughing ruefully, tossing aside his briefcase, a stack of newspapers and then a bunch of flowers so that his arms were free and he could pull her to him. He kissed her soundly and then looked into her face with smiling eyes.

He looked so big, and so handsome in his business suit, that all Araminta's doubts and fears melted away in the rightness of being with him.

'Oh, Steven,' she said laughing,

pulling him into the kitchen, 'you must be exhausted! Let me fix you a drink. What would you like? Were you stuck in the traffic jam? Darling, I'm so pleased to see you. But, about dinner . . . '

9

Despite the flowers, the soothing decor, and the soft music that wafted around the waiting-room, the place was unmistakably a hospital. Araminta swallowed hard.

She leaned her aching head on the pale blue wall behind her.

A glamorous female, who was, nevertheless, unmistakably a nurse, clicked briskly over the polished floor towards Araminta.

'Mr Sparkle will see you now,' she said.

She looked bored, and whirled away without waiting to see if Araminta followed her. Araminta's heart was pounding as she fumbled for the bag, scarf and coat she had put down beside her. She rose to her feet and hurriedly followed the nurse's starched back along the polished corridors of the private hospital. Her mind had gone blank, and she could think of none of the fine logical speeches she had prepared earlier.

The nurse came to a stop by a door, tapped on it sharply, and turned away without speaking again. The voice that came from inside was low, but clear.

'Come in.'

Araminta pushed the door open halfway. She saw that her hand was shaking badly. She wanted to turn tail and run away, but she comforted herself with the thought that nothing Fred Sparkle could say to her could make her more miserable than she already was. On that cheerful note she pushed the door fully open and went in.

The man who was lying propped up on the pillows looked nothing like a pop star. His blue pyjamas were wrinkled. The sad lines of his face made him look tired and listless. He was gaunt rather than fashionably thin, and his lank black hair showed a two inch re-growth of sandy grey roots. He eyed Araminta with very little interest.

'The romantic picture seeker,' he said, his voice holding an exhausted note.

Araminta crossed the room quickly and shook his head. All her expectations of a spoiled, self-indulgent pop-star faded away. This man looked as if he'd been through the mill. Her sympathetic, nurturing instincts came to the fore as she smiled down at him.

'How are you?'

He shrugged and turned away.

'All right.'

'I guess that means convalescent,' Araminta said cheerfully.

He looked back at her, a faint spark of interest in his eyes.

'What do you mean?'

'No interesting symptoms to tell me about, but not feeling well either,' she explained as she pulled out the visitor's chair and sat down. 'In our family, we called this stage the don't-feel-likes.'

One corner of the pop star's mouth turned upwards.

'The what?'

Araminta chanted, 'Don't feel like getting up! Don't feel like staying in bed! Don't feel like watching TV.'

Fred Sparkle chimed in, laughing.

'Don't feel like any dinner! Don't feel like reading a book! Oh, I know just what you mean.'

Araminta smiled at him.

'It was very good of you to see me. I hope you feel like having visitors.'

His blue eyes were warm and his expression quite awake now.

'I do when they make me feel as good as you do. I haven't had much to laugh about recently.'

'I'm sorry,' Araminta said.

Fred didn't seem to want to dwell on his troubles. He changed the subject.

'Hasn't Steven come with you? I was surprised when the nurse just gave your name.'

Araminta's cheeks glowed red and she dropped her lashes over her eyes to veil the misery in them.

'I don't think Steven and I will be

doing much together in future.'

Fred sat up on one elbow and looked at her sharply.

'No? I thought you two were in love! Steven certainly was. I never saw a man so smitten. He was raving about you. What happened?'

The pain that twisted Araminta's stomach was sickening.

'Steven in love with me? I don't think so! He wouldn't have wanted me to change so much if that was the case.'

Fred gave her a wise look, but he didn't try to argue with her. He just spoke quietly.

'There are always adjustments to be made when two people come together, on both sides.'

Araminta shook her head.

'He wanted me to do all the changing.'

Fred's smile made his blue eyes shine, and Araminta felt the strength of his personality for the first time. Suddenly she could believe that he was a star.

'Well, that's no good, then,' he said. 'It's got to be two-way to work. You find someone who'll appreciate you for exactly who you are. That's the recipe for happiness.'

Araminta's heart was distraught at the very idea of finding someone else. She knew that she would never want anyone but Steven. It had been the darkest hour of her life when she told him that she wanted to end their relationship.

Fred's head fell back on the pillows and his tone was suddenly exhausted.

'Only once you've found that person, don't ever let them go, Araminta. Life's no good without them.'

For a moment, she thought Fred was referring to her and Steven, but then she saw a tear trickle down one cheek. She took one of his cold, thin hands between her warm ones.

'Is that what happened to you?' she asked gently.

He was silent for a moment, then he turned his head towards her. There was a bleak, hopeless expression in his eyes.

'She died,' Fred said simply. 'That surprises you, doesn't it? Nobody knew I had a love in my life.'

'You lost your partner?'

Now the expression in those blue eyes was desperate.

'Yes, and I can't carry on without her. I can't. Life isn't worth living. It's ironic. I went through the agony of the recovery programme because I knew I was slowly killing myself. But now I'm through it all, I don't want to live anyway.'

Araminta didn't know what to say for the best. Fred turned his head away from her with a petulant motion, and she was afraid that she was going to fail him. She could at least try to keep him talking. She asked the first question that came into her head.

'Why did you keep your love affair such a secret?'

'I keep asking myself that,' Fred said, looking at her sadly. 'Now it's too late. Now I realise how much she meant to me, I wish I'd shouted our love from the rooftops. I was a fool. My manager convinced me that I'd lose fans if they knew about my romance. What do a few record sales mean compared with the fact that she's gone? I wish everybody had known her.'

'They still could.'

His head swung round to her and his gaze was sharp.

'What do you mean?'

Her tone was hesitant. It was difficult for her to express her true feelings, but she felt that she wanted to help this man.

'Don't the best songs come from sad experiences?' she began slowly. 'You have such a gift, Fred, with your music. Why don't you throw aside what your manager thinks will be popular? Kill off the old Fred Sparkle, the false one. Write songs that are true to your heart.'

She broke off, feeling that Fred was no longer listening to her. For a moment she was worried that her helpful ideas had been rejected, but then he put one hand on her arm and she saw that his eyes were blazing with passion.

'A memorial! I'll write the most beautiful songs of my life, and I'll dedicate the album to Lisa.'

Araminta felt caught up in his excitement. Anything seemed possible.

'That way, she could live on for ever,' she agreed. 'People would know about her and remember her.'

Fred pushed aside the bedclothes and lowered his weak legs to the floor.

'I was on the right track wanting to kill someone,' he said cheerfully, his whole face alight. 'Fred Sparkle is dead. Long live the new Fred Sparkle!'

He leaned over and enveloped Araminta in a massive hug. Then he pulled back and regarded her with warm, serious eyes.

'Will you come and see me again?' he asked.

'Of course I will,' Araminta said warmly, 'I'd like to.'

Fred got back into bed. He looked

tired, but calm and peaceful.

'Was this just a social visit,' he enquired, 'or is there something I can do for you?'

Araminta hesitated. Her request seemed very trivial. She was about to deny it, but Fred had been watching her face.

'Spit it out! Remember, you have just given me an idea to pull me back from the brink, really. There isn't much I wouldn't do for you now.'

'Well,' she admitted, 'you know you're having Thornclough Manor gutted.'

'Go on.'

'Well, I was wondering if you would mind my salvaging the stained-glass screen in the library. It's such a beautiful piece. I can't bear to think of it being destroyed. I'd like to restore it.'

Fred was already reaching for his mobile phone. It only took him a few seconds to get through the site manager and arrange for Araminta to have the screen. Promising to fax confirmation later, he hung up.

'Sure that's all you want?' he asked. 'Few thousand quid? Use of my motor car? You name it, it's yours.'

'That's all I want,' Araminta said. 'Thank you, Fred.'

He looked totally exhausted. Knowing he needed to rest, she got up to leave. The smile he gave her was brilliant, but more importantly, it was happy and resolved.

'On the contrary,' Fred said, and the deep husky vibrancy that had made him famous was back in his voice. 'It's me who should thank you.'

Araminta was so deep in thought as she left the hospital, that, although she noticed the man in a dark jacket who was sheltering under the weeping willows that lined the hospital grounds, she didn't realise it was Steven until he had crossed the lawn and was standing right in front of her. He blocked her way, and she had to stop.

Araminta raised her eyes and searched Steven's face. It was drawn and there were new lines around his eyes and mouth. His eyes were unreadable dark shadows. His coat collar was turned up against the light spring rain, and rain glistened in his hair.

'I don't know if I'm surprised to find you here or not,' he said, gesturing her to continue towards the gate and falling into step beside her. 'First I made a list of all the logical places you might be, but then my intuition told me to come here.'

He put a hand on her arm to guide her the way he wanted her to go. Araminta responded to the slight pressure he put on her arm and turned left. They began to follow the path that followed the boundary wall of the hospital. Made from red brick, the wall was high enough to block out the sights and sounds of the city behind. A flowerbed lay below the wall. The damp earth smelled good. Fine water drops frosted the delicate spring growth of new leaves and fresh green.

Araminta felt dazed.

'You followed your heart,' she said softly, very conscious of him beside her.

He paused and looked down at her. The love in his eyes was dizzying.

'I followed my heart because it told me never to rest until I'd found you and made you mine. Darling Minty, will you marry me?'

For a long moment she stood frozen, looking at him, but then she pulled away and carried on walking. Steven was forced to follow her or fall behind.

'Whose name would I take?' she asked softly.

His voice and expression showed his surprise.

'Why mine, of course.'

Tears weren't far away as she questioned him softly.

'Whose house would we live in?'

Now impatience tinged his tone.

'What objections could you possibly have to my flat?'

Her heart was like lead in her chest, but she forced herself to continue. She stopped and looked at him very openly.

'What kind of lifestyle would we have?'

Steven brushed aside her concern.

'A normal kind of lifestyle! What does all this have to do with you and me?'

Could she make him understand? Ignoring the rain that was now running down her face, Araminta tried to explain.

'Steven, I feel as if you're swallowing me up. I'd lose my name, my roots, my home, my way of life.'

He broke in impatiently.

'I don't want to hear this, Araminta! All I want is to make you happy. What's so bad about that? I'll give you anything you want.'

She looked down. Her vision was blurred, perhaps by the rain. Then she looked up. Her heart was breaking as she spoke the words.

'I want the freedom to be an artist.'

Steven caught up both her forearms in his hands and actually shook them in his effort to convince her to see things his way.

'You can be an artist! You can be anything you want. I'm not the kind of old-fashioned ogre that wants to keep the little woman at home. I found you a studio. Would I have done that if I hadn't wanted you to be an artist?'

The intensity of his gaze was hard to resist, but she persisted bravely.

'I couldn't work with Mr Tamworth. He only cares about profit.'

A coldness was appearing on Steven's face now.

'You just turn down all my arrangements without thinking about them, Araminta. Last night you accused me of not being interested in any kind of compromise. Well, I thought about what you said, and I realised that you would be giving up your security, although I don't think you could describe the dump you were living in as secure. But if you come to live with me, you will be making a big move, and so, to show you how serious I am,

I'm offering to marry you. What more could you want?'

Her emotions choked her, but she managed to say in a low voice, 'A marriage is about teamwork and partnership. I appreciate that you feel as if you're offering me a lot.'

'More than I've ever offered any other woman!' he broke in.

Araminta started at him earnestly, willing him to understand.

'But I can't be happy with a man who doesn't take me seriously, who won't listen to me. You don't value the same things I do, and I can't accept that.'

Steven stared at her blankly, and she felt that she was looking into the face of a stranger.

'Value? You can't seriously tell me that you value living in that funny old village in that uncomfortable old house?'

He broke off and stared incredulously at the tears welling up in her eyes.

'What?' he demanded in exasperation. 'Just tell me what there is to value about being poor and burying yourself in the country?'

Araminta was crying in earnest now, and Steven suddenly seemed to notice that the rain, which had been getting steadily heavier for some time, was now falling steadily.

'Oh, this is hopeless!' he snarled, pushing wet hair off his forehead with an impatient gesture. 'For goodness' sake, Araminta, let's get out of this downpour and go somewhere we can talk. You have to listen to me, you have to let me explain.'

'Explain why I should see things your way?' she enquired, looking up at him sadly. 'It'll never work, Steven.'

And, putting one hand up to stem the sobs that threatened to engulf her, she turned on her heel and raced blindly away from the man she loved.

★   ★   ★

The sky outside Fred Sparkle's room was brilliantly blue, and the air that poured in through the open window was sweet with the promise of spring. Spring seemed to have touched the heart of the man who lay on the bed. He looked completely different from the man Araminta had visited two days ago.

'I'm so glad that you're writing music again, Fred,' Araminta said, pushing a tumbling curl behind her ear with one fine delicate hand, and smiling at the sheets of scribbled music that lay scattered all around the room. 'I'm sure that your new songs are going to be the best you have ever written. Writing again is also a sign that you're getting better, that you'll recover.'

'Thanks to you,' Fred said. 'I'll always miss Lisa, you know. There'll never be any one else for me, but somehow, through my music, I feel like I can make sense of what happened.'

'You'll help other people, too,'

Araminta said, and then she added shyly, 'Your music is so wonderful. It's helped me in the past. You have the gift of touching people's hearts.'

Laughter put sunshine into the famous voice.

'A fan! Darling Minty, you'll have to give me a chance to see your work. Maybe we can form a mutual appreciation society. You'll have to let me look at the panel you're restoring. I might want to buy it back off you.'

And then he looked at her face.

'What have I said? What are you looking so pleased about?'

Araminta hugged her arms around herself.

'You know, I went to Thornclough Manor to get the panel,' she began slowly, stopping and smiling at the memory.

'Go on!' Fred demanded, sitting bolt upright on his pillows.

'The site manager had been too busy to notice it,' Araminta continued, 'so I went with him into the library. He called a couple of workmen. He wouldn't let me touch anything because of insurance, but said I had better instruct them as to the best way to remove the panel. Anyway, I told them, and very carefully, one of them began collecting up the broken chips of glass that were scattered around and the other one began prising the panel out of the chimney breast.'

'Will you get on with it!' Fred demanded.

'And behind the panel, fallen down at the back, was my picture.'

The famous blue eyes blazed with interest.

'No!'

Araminta nodded happily, reliving the incredible moment in her memory.

'It was dusty, of course, but undamaged. The strained-glass panel had protected it from the worst of the dirt and decay. It had been just lying there for all those years, waiting.'

'Waiting for what?' Fred enquired, fairly bouncing on the bed in his interest. 'What are you going to do with it?'

'I didn't know at first,' Araminta. 'I rang up the national Portrait Gallery because they were the last people to ask for the painting to be in a show. They advised me to take it to one of the big auction houses so that their experts could carry out any necessary restoration. And they are going to value it for me, and arrange the sale.'

Fred's blue eyes were incredulous.

'Sell your mother's picture! After all the hours you spent looking for it? I don't get this at all.'

Araminta looked down at the hands that were twisting in her lap, but her eyes were calm when she raised them to meet the snapping blue of Fred Sparkle's gaze.

'It was a hard decision to make,' she admitted, 'but I thought it over very carefully, and I'm sure I've made the right decision. The art expert said that one of the national galleries would probably buy it, because Camille

Barton is such a popular artist. That would mean that my mother's picture would be on display where everyone could see it, not just me. I think I'd like that. I think mother would have liked that, too, and Camille. She hated to think of the picture mouldering away unseen.'

And then Araminta gazed at the pop star. Her voice took on an earnest note.

'And, Fred, there's something I need the money for. Something very important.'

His sharp gaze met hers.

'Now why do I get the feeling that I'm involved in all this somehow?'

'I'm sorry, Fred, and of course you have the right to say no, but I have to ask you.'

Araminta raised her pleading eyes to meet his blue gaze before voicing her request.

'I want to buy back my family home. I want to restore Thornclough Manor to its natural beauty. It's a Regency house and I want to keep it that way, Fred.'

'And where would I live if you bought the roof from over my head?' Fred grumbled.

Araminta whipped out a pile of glossy brochures from her handbag.

'Why don't you take a look at these?' she said innocently. 'Steven recommends this company. He says they do the best conversions in the North. He bought his own apartment from them.'

Fred was laughing as he began flicking through the elegant pictures.

'I get the feeling I'm being set up here,' he complained.

Araminta was too tense to realise that she was being teased. Her words poured out in an impassioned flood.

'Oh, Fred, do think about it, please. I was talking to the site manager. Things haven't gone too far. I could still make the manor the beautiful place it used to be. It seems so wasteful to spend all that money forcing Thornclough to be something that it's not. And just look at those pictures. Industrial property is perfect for what you want. There's space, and light, and you could live next to the water and — '

'And that's enough!' Fred commanded, his face stern.

Araminta bit back the tirade of words she still had to say and felt her heart sink. She had gone too far and annoyed him. Her lashes fell softly over her eyes as if to shut out unpleasant reality, and then they lifted and she faced him bravely.

'I'm sorry, Fred. Thornclough is yours to do with as you please.'

'And what pleases me,' the pop star cut in, grinning, 'is to sell it back to you. I've got no emotional investment in the place. I've never even seen it.'

He shook the glossy brochure.

'One of these places would suit me just as well. Better in fact. Since I've been feeling better, I've been thinking about the future. I'm not going back to London, not just yet, anyway. I told

Steven to find me a quiet place in the country, but now I think about it, central Manchester would be more convenient than a little village like yours.'

'Really?' Araminta breathed, staring hopefully into his blue eyes.

He nodded firmly.

'Really. You choose me one of these places, only make sure it'll be ready to move into next week. I want to get out of here as soon as possible.'

Araminta's voice went so high that it squeaked.

'Me chose a place for you? I couldn't!'

The blue eyes glimmered.

'You'll find me a nice place, girl.' Then he laughed. 'From all you've told me about you and modern houses, all you have to do is choose the one you hate most!'

Araminta opened the brochure and said, 'You'll have to give me some idea of which one you like. What are you looking for?'

Fred shoved the brochure back at her.

'I like them all,' he said cheerfully, 'and I haven't got time to go shopping. Just don't spent more than three million pounds, all right?'

'Three million pounds?' Araminta squeaked.

Fred picked up his mobile phone and showed her a button.

'Link to the site manager at Thornclough manor,' he explained cheerfully. 'If you want me to ring him and call off the demolition process, you have to agree to choose a new house for me.'

There's no choice, Araminta thought, and it might even be fun.

'Phone him,' she said firmly. 'I'll find you a house, Fred. You can call off the demolition.'

10

This has to be the first day of summer,'
Araminta said, tipping up her face to
enjoy the sunshine. 'What a glorious
day for a picnic.'

'Don't get sunburned,' Fred warned,
looking at her creamy skin.

'I won't. I've got sunblock on.'

She smiled at him.

'I'm so glad you could come, Fred.
You look like a different person!'

The famous blue eyes twinkled.

'I thought you looked surprised when
I arrived. I wondered at first if I'd come
on the right Saturday, but I knew you
were expecting me. We've talked on the
phone every day this week. Am I so
changed?'

'You look great,' Araminta told him.

She decided that she had better not
explain that subconsciously she had
obviously been expecting the pale,

washed-out invalid that she had first met. It had been a real shock to find a living, breathing pop star on her doorstep. And now Fred was better, he looked every inch the star he was.

He lay back on the red tartan rug that was spread across the centre of the lawn in front of Thornclough Manor.

'I feel great,' he said simply.

Then he rolled over and gazed at the exterior of the half-gutted house.

'Are you sure I didn't give the order to stop work too late? This place is a bomb site.'

Araminta shook her head firmly.

'It's all right. A lot would have had to come out anyway, to allow for dry-rot treatment, and new plumbing, and a new roof, and modern wiring and everything else that it needs.'

'You're crazy,' Fred said laughing. 'I can't think why you don't buy yourself a nicely-done apartment like mine.'

Araminta met his eyes anxiously.

'You do like your new place, then?'

There was no mistaking the sincerity in his tone.

'I love it! As soon as I walked in, it felt like home. You couldn't have chosen a better place. Which reminds me, has the Press been here?'

'Press?' Araminta questioned, her eyes wide with surprise. 'Why should the Press come here? I didn't tell anyone that you were coming.'

Fred gave her a reassuring smile.

'I know you wouldn't have, but I'm afraid someone has been indiscreet about the house purchase. Your name is in all the papers, linked with mine.'

'My name?' Araminta gasped in horror.

'Sorry, darling, but there's nothing they love more than to make up stories about my love life. Someone has told them that it was one sexy Araminta Shaw who carried out all the arrangements for my new flat, and they've gone and made a wedding out of it.'

'That's ridiculous!'

'I know, but that's the way it goes.'

Fred gave her an uncertain look.

'And, if you don't mind, I'd like to keep the Lisa thing to myself, at least until the album comes out.'

Araminta smiled at him.

'If any reporters do come, I'll tell the truth about me and I won't mention Lisa. If they don't believe me, well, they'll just look very silly later on.'

Fred's eyes betrayed his relief.

'I'm still a bit raw,' he admitted. 'I couldn't talk about it in public yet.'

Araminta put one hand on Fred's arm. She was about to say something sympathetic, she wasn't sure what, but Fred cut off her words by leaping to his feet and yelling. A small brown bundle fell to the ground. Fred gazed at the round ball in disgust.

'It's one of your pesky hedgehogs!' he yelled. 'It was climbing up my stomach.'

'I'm sorry,' Araminta said, struggling to keep a straight face. 'That's Storming Norman, the biggest baby. He's very inquisitive and he loves to explore.'

The brown spiny ball uncurled itself

and two button bright eyes twinkled up at Fred. The pop star gazed down at the small animal that stood on the bright tartan rug looking cheekily back at him. Then he suddenly burst out laughing. He addressed the young hedgehog sternly.

'Ask before you try that again, lad.'

Araminta was glad to be able to laugh with Fred.

'Perhaps I shouldn't have brought them to our picnic,' she admitted, chuckling. 'But they do so love an outing.'

Fred shook his head at the empty cat basket that sat in the middle of a patch of green grass and daisies.

'Eccentric, that's what she is,' he said to the blue summer sky. 'I don't know any other woman who carries a basket full of hedgehogs around with her!'

'Cheer up,' Araminta said, still laughing. 'I carried a second basket, too, and that's full of food and drink.'

She passed Fred a glass of ice-cold,

sparkling water and they chinked glasses solemnly.

'To your album,' she said.

'And your house,' Fred replied. 'How is the restoration going?'

'Still at the planning stage,' Araminta admitted, sitting back on the rug in the warm sunshine and wishing she could picnic outside every day. 'Technically, I don't even own the manor yet, but I come here every day to take notes and decide on the future.'

Fred looked concerned.

'Is there any problem? Can I help?'

Araminta was quick to reassure him.

'Thank you, but there's no problem. I just have to wait for my picture to be auctioned. Once I've got the money, all the paperwork can be sorted out, and once I truly own Thornclough, the restoration can begin.'

'It seems a slow business,' Fred grumbled. 'You don't have to wait until you can give me the money. I trust you. Why don't you start at once?'

Araminta smiled at him.

'That's sweet of you, Fred, but I don't know if the builders would be as trusting. And to be honest, I'm not ready to begin. I'd like plenty of time to think things over before I make any big decisions.'

'Wise,' Fred murmured, watching her as she unpacked the basket. 'Oh, those pastry things look good. What's in them? Mushrooms?'

'Yes, those are mushroom and the others are cheese and here are some with shrimp,' Araminta said, taking the hint and passing Fred the vol-au-vents she had made earlier.

'I didn't know it could be so nice out in the country,' Fred said, chewing blissfully and looking around him. 'What are those yellow flower thingies in the lawn called?'

'You are a Londoner.'

Araminta laughed, helping herself to a sausage roll.

'They are called dandelions, and any self-respecting gardener would be ashamed to have them in a lawn.'

'Why? I think they look nice. Sort of cheery.'

He was interrupted by Araminta's hedgehogs, who had been happily exploring around the lawn. Now they seemed to have smelled the food. All four of them arrived in haste and stood on the edge of the rug, noses twitching greedily.

'Oh, no, you don't, maties,' Fred said. 'Araminta's cooking is too good for you.'

'I've got them a tin of their favourite cat food,' Araminta began, reaching into the basket.

And then she heard a car engine — a familiar six-cylinder car engine. Still clutching the tin-opener, she stared at Fred accusingly.

'You didn't?'

He stared back with honest bewilderment in his blue eyes.

'Didn't what?'

Even when Steven's green Range Rover appeared around the bend in the drive, Fred didn't react until Steven himself stepped out on to the gravel. As soon as the pop star recognised Steven, a broad smile reached his lips.

'Ah,' Fred said enigmatically, 'I wondered if this would happen.'

'What?' Araminta questioned frantically. 'What?'

She felt overwhelmed by confusion. The mouthful of flaky pastry that had seemed so delicious only seconds ago dried to sawdust in her mouth, and she swallowed it mechanically. Her heart was beating in uneven jerks.

11

Her eyes locked on to the dear, familiar form of Steven. She realised all over again how much she had missed him, how she had longed for him every second of the days that they had been apart.

Steven began to move towards them, slowly and uncertainly. Araminta thought her heart would choke her.

'Don't mind me,' Fred said.

He turned away from Araminta and picked up the guitar that he had brought along with him. He bent over it and began to play a tune that Araminta hardly heard. Her whole being was focused on the man who was slowly moving towards her. She stood up to meet him.

'Hi,' she said uncertainly.

She sneaked a glance at him, then looked away. The impact of meeting the brightness of those well-remembered grey eyes was devastating. Steven's eyes met hers briefly, then slid away and focused on Fred.

'Hi,' he said, still looking at the pop star.

He'd lost weight. Araminta felt the urge to fuss over him and feed him up. She didn't like the hollows in his cheekbones or the gaunt look about his face. He was wearing the mouse-grey corduroy trousers and white Aran sweater he had worn on that weekend so long ago, and she wished fiercely that she still had the right to fling herself into his arms and bury herself in his chest.

She half held out her hand to take Steven's, but then she realised that she was still holding the tin-opener, so she changed the movement into an airy gesture towards the picnic rug.

'Won't you sit down?' she asked unsteadily.

Steven folded his long length on to the tartan rug without saying anything.

There was no wine, in deference to Fred's recovery, so Araminta bent her head over the picnic basket, making the excuse of finding a bottle of sparkling water. She wanted to hide her extreme agitation. Not looking at Steven properly, she handed him a crystal glass that sparkled and fizzed in the sunshine.

He took it with a murmured word that turned into a cough. Meanwhile Fred continued to bend over his guitar, strumming a plaintive and oddly haunting tune.

Araminta put her arms around her knees and hugged them, almost as if she were one of her hedgehog babies, unconsciously curling her body up for protection against the tension in the atmosphere. She gazed into the distance, trying to ignore the man who sat beside her. The wind sighed gently in the fresh green tops of the trees that ran along the boundary of the lawn.

Sitting low down on the lawn like this, the grey houses of the village vanished into the fold of the valley, but the bulk of Pendle Hill was clearly visible, looking very near in the sunshine. The blue sky behind the hill seemed to hold the perfection of summer.

The tense silence was broken by the sound of another engine. This one was a great deal smaller than Steven's Range Rover. It sounded like the light, steady purring of a sewing machine. Fred continued to be absorbed in the music he was creating on the guitar, but both Steven and Araminta, relieved to have somewhere to look, turned towards the drive and watched the bright yellow moped that puttered to a halt in front of the manor.

A slim young girl in her late teens swung herself off the moped, took off her helmet and shook out her trendily-cut hair. She seemed completely unconscious of any awkwardness in the atmosphere. She came over to the picnic rug at a dash, laughing and talking at once.

'I'm not too late, am I? I hope you

saved me some shrimps, Minty.'

She turned to Steven and gave him a broad grin.

'I have a thing about shrimps!' she informed him solemnly, before falling on the picnic basket and rummaging around for her favourite tit-bit.

Steven tore his fascinated gaze from her and raised his eyebrows questioningly at Araminta. She blushed. Why did Steven always make her blush so? Then she pulled herself together enough to introduce the young girl.

'Steven, this is Laura, my new assistant,' she told him.

His grey eyes flew open wide in startled enquiry. Araminta met his look honestly.

'I took your advice,' she admitted. 'I think it's going to work out well.'

Laura interrupted her chewing long enough to say, 'Great chance for me. Now there's no grants or nothing. I could never go to college, but Minty's cool. She even lent me the money for my moped.'

A deep happiness suffused Steven's grey eyes and he leaned towards Araminta impulsively.

'Minty, darling,' he began, but then he seemed to catch hold of himself and draw back, clearing his throat. 'I'm glad,' he said formally. 'And that reminds me of another thing to be glad about. I actually came here to congratulate you both, Araminta and Fred, on your wedding, and to give you my very warmest wishes for your happiness in the future.'

A fleeting look of pain crossed his face then Laura spluttered and choked over her shrimp vol-au-vent.

Fred struck a discordant note on his guitar and burst out laughing. Araminta sat dumbstruck in the midst of the chaos, twisting her hands together. It was an effort to lift her eyes to Steven's face.

'That's just newspaper nonsense, Steven. There's no truth in it.'

His face went very still.

'No? I had it from an associate of

mine that you were choosing Fred's new house.'

'Well, yes, I did,' Araminta said slowly. 'It was the least I could do after throwing Fred out of Thornclough, but it doesn't mean anything.'

Dawning hope warred with disbelief in Steven's eyes, and his conflicting emotions choked his voice as he said, 'Then there's nothing between you?'

'Nothing but friendship,' Araminta said, realising even as she spoke that Fred was proving just what a good friend he was by collecting up rampaging hedgehogs.

Laura was busy wrestling with the tin-opener. A strong smell of fish pervaded the air as she succeeded in opening it, and the hedgehogs waded in happily.

Steven drew Araminta slightly away and spoke to her privately.

'I was lying,' he said bluntly. 'I didn't come to congratulate you on marrying Fred. I came to stop you any way I could. You must never marry anyone but me, Minty.'

As she met the dizzying tenderness in his eyes, Araminta's heart melted within her. As she raised her face towards his, Steven pressed one gentle finger to her lips.

'Wait, darling,' he said softly, 'let me finish. It's not easy. I'm still confused, but when I saw the newspapers . . . '

Araminta was close enough to him to feel the shudder that ran through his whole body as he said the words. He looked at her earnestly, willing her to understand.

'I've been so miserable since you've gone. I thought at first it was just because you'd gone, because I'd lost my girlfriend, but it was more than that, Minty. I missed the way we'd been together.'

She looked at him closely, startled, unable to believe what she was hearing. He nodded tenderly and brushed her cheek with caressing fingers.

'Girlfriends have come and gone in my life before, and it's never meant much. Miss 'em for a few days and then carry on as normal, but you, Minty, when you left it was as if a hole had been torn in my life and nothing was any good any more.'

One arm crept around her, and she stole closer to his warm chest in the soft white sweater as he continued.

'Everything seemed to be sterile, empty, and that's when I realised that it was because my life was sterile and empty. It had been for a long time. I don't know if you'll believe this, after all the time I spent complaining, but I missed the quality of life in your village. I didn't want to live behind glazed windows any more. I missed the smell of log fires and the way that they crackle. I missed your generous, messy toast and the best marmalade in the world.'

His arms gathered her up in a warm, crushing hug.

'And then I was arrogant enough to expect you to give up your wonderful way of life for the great prize of marrying me. I can't believe what a fool I was. I was completely wrong.'

His eyes darkened and his voice took on a deeply serious note.

'Minty, darling, the biggest favour a man could hope to win would be you consenting to be his wife. Now that I've come to my senses and realised this, I hardly dare ask you, but will you marry me, darling?'

It was the great sunburst of happiness exploding in Araminta's heart that silenced her for a moment, but Steven hastened to convince her of his change of heart.

'Let me live with you, in your village, your way,' he continued, a pleading light in his eyes.

'Oh, Steven.'

Araminta sighed, finding her voice and gazing up at him lovingly. She pushed back her curls.

'There's nothing I'd like more, and you are not the only one who was wrong. I've been thinking about what you said about being more businesslike, and you were right. You were right about taking an apprentice like Laura, and I'm sure you were right about other things, too. I hope you were right! I've got all kinds of plans for Thornclough, and some of them are very expensive indeed.'

A kiss as soft as a sunbeam landed on the tip of her nose.

'Together,' he promised her, 'we'll build a real family home at Thornclough. The manor will be restored to its former beauty and we'll live happily ever afterwards.'

His lips met hers gently to seal the pact. Araminta melted into his embrace knowing that she had truly come home at last. She was safe in Steven's arms, and was only dimly aware of the excited reaction of her friends.

'And Laura's going to get to be a bridesmaid at your wedding,' Araminta's young apprentice said enthusiastically. 'Cool! I've always wanted to do that.'

Steven raised his head briefly, just

long enough to say, 'Do you know any good picture framers? I've already booked a copy of Camille Barton's picture. It's better for the original to be in a gallery, free for all to enjoy, but I want my very own picture of happiness hanging over the fireplace.'

'I'll see to that.' Fred grinned. 'It'll be my wedding present to you both.'

Still smiling widely, the world-famous pop star picked up his guitar and began to strum it. He played a few notes at random, and then settled down into the song he thought best fitted the occasion.

The orphan hedgehogs ran freely over the lush summer lawn, crystal glasses clinked gaily as Laura insisted they all drank a toast, and Araminta knew that she had never been happier, as Fred picked off the last triumphant notes of Here Comes the Bride.

CONVALESCENT HEART

Lynne Collins

They called Romily the Snow Queen, but once she had been all fire and passion, kindled into loving by a man's kiss and sure it would last a lifetime. She still believed it would, for her. It had lasted only a few months for the man who had stormed into her heart. After Greg, how could she trust any man again? So was it likely that surgeon Jake Conway could pierce the icy armour that the lovely ward sister had wrapped about her emotions?